THE
Orphan
AND THE
King

⚜

Volume II

Love's Great Ransom

By
Wendy Anne Hunt

Library of Congress Control: 2008906229
      Hunt, Wendy A.
            The Orphan and the King: Love's Great Ransom/by Wendy Hunt.
            ISBN - 13: 978-0-9814561-2-6
            ISBN - 10: 0-9814561-2-X

Cover photo copyrights iStockphoto.com

Edited by **Kristen Diaz**
Assistant Editor: **Laura Williams**
Cover Design and Interior Layout by **Catherine Lackey**
Cover Photos by **Jaimie Miller** and **Bob Buchan**
Models: **Tim Wolf, Connor Hunt, Bekah Buchan**
Interior Illustrations by **Alphonso A. Cornelius**
Costumes by **Trish Reichfeld**

Published by Hunt & Peck Press
Printed in the United States of America
2010

WendyAnneHunt@comcast.net
www.HuntandPeckPress.com

Preface

"In You the orphan finds mercy." Hosea 14:3

I found myself on my knees, weeping and burdened for children I didn't know, and probably would never meet, but God knew each one by name.

It was June, 1999. My husband had left just days before for a mission trip to Juarez, Mexico. Their purpose was to build a playground for an orphanage, minister to the children, preach the Gospel in the surrounding area, and support the local church.

After putting our eleven-month-old down for an afternoon nap, I went to my knees before the Lord to intercede for my husband and the others on his team. What the Lord did in my own heart during that time was unanticipated, and became the inspiration for this book.

The Lord broke my heart with His heart for the fatherless. What welled up in my heart was the desire to write a short story that would reveal to them the special place they hold in the heart of our Father God.

Ten years later, the 'short story' has evolved into a novel, but the heart behind it has remained throughout. As Psalms 68:5 so clearly states, He is truly the "Father of the fatherless."

Another desire of my heart is that God would, in some small way, use this allegorical re-telling of 'His-story' to draw many hearts closer to the Savior. I want people to *know* my sweet Jesus. I want them to know a Jesus who wept with the hurting. But I also want them to see a picture of a Jesus who was good-natured and even light-hearted at times. I want to give them a glimpse of a Jesus who laughed with the joyful, who loved and played with the little children, and whose face often bore a smile because His heart was filled with joy. Although movies about the life of Christ portray Him as humorless, somber, and solemn, it only makes sense that the fruits of the Spirit, of which joy is one, would be embodied in the One who created them!

My prayer is that many would encounter Him afresh, if not for the very first time, within the pages of this book.

Dedication

I would like to dedicate this book to:

My wonderful, patient and supportive husband, Kevin, and three children...for the many sacrifices they made so that I could finish this endeavor!

My Editor, Kristen Diaz, for a job well done. You are an amazing woman and a very talented editor. What an absolute god-send you were to me. How you edited a book being legally blind -- I still can't get my head around it! Kristen, you simply *amaze* me!!! Thank you!

My Project Coordinator and Layout Editor, Catherine Lackey, who helped with so very many aspects of pulling this book together -- thanks, my friend!

My models (Tim Wolf, Connor Hunt, and Bekah Buchan) and photographers (Jaimie Miller and Bob Buchan), who endured freezing weather and *outlandish* requests just to get the 'perfect shot'! Thank you...You guys were GREAT!!!

Alphonso Cornelius, illustrator extraordinaire, whose vision, expertise and encouragement I am so grateful for!

Katie and Scott Farris for assisting with your input on this book, thank you for your wise advice and skillful critique, as well as your encouragement and support! And to all of my junior advisors whose input and unique perspective were invaluable: Bradley Honsinger, Philip Baillie, and Connor Hunt. Thank you!

The loving memory of Emerson King. A true giant in the kingdom of God, he laid aside all the accomplishments of this world in order to live a simple life for the glory of God. We were privileged, as he walked among us for a while, to have rubbed shoulders with this man. He was the greatest warrior I have ever met, and won many a battle on his calloused knees. May we take up the humble mantle of prayer now where our brother left off, may we carry the burdens of others selflessly upon our hearts as he carried so many of ours, and may we, too, accomplish mighty exploits in the service of our King, on our knees!

and lastly...

Orphaned children the world over, that they may know the special place they hold in the heart of their heavenly father.

TABLE OF CONTENTS

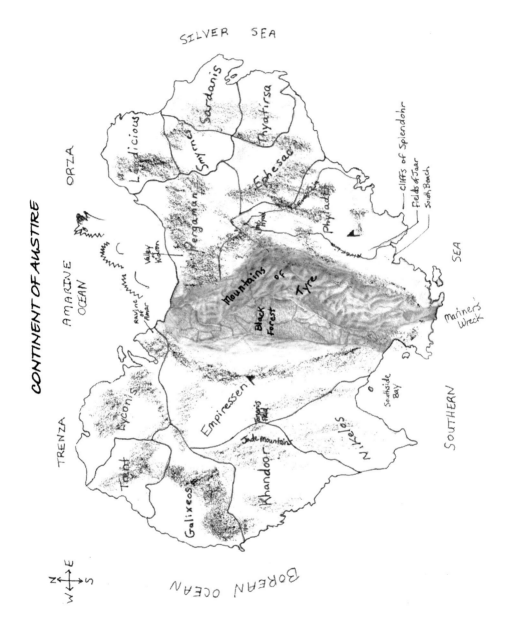

MAIN CHARACTER DESCRIPTIONS

Emperor Liam – Reagale's father, the great Emperor beyond the Silver Sea

King Reagale Constance - Ruler of all the provinces of Orza

Wesley - A young boy from the city of Trenza

Gabriella - Wesley's mother

Connor - One of King Reagale's court officials and a trusted friend and Comrade

Brianna – Connor's sister and another of the King's most trusted and loyal subjects, as well as a dear friend

Christias - Another of the King's court officials and loyal friends

Limpett, Norpid and Truffle - Three dwarf brothers, they are also court officials for Reagale and among the closest to Him

Lord Darius - The evil ruler of the provinces of Trenza

Troan - An unusual winged being, and faithful messenger, as well as dearest friend throughout the years to both Reagale and Liam

Kavin – Captain of the Guard for the King's army, and member of the inner court

Silver – King Reagale's Horse

Nibbles – Wesley's Pony

Trey, Tameric, Abdi, Doctor Emerson, Finley – The remaining members of the King's inner court

General Lanos – Leader of Darius' army

Zantar – Spy Darius secretly sent to infiltrate the palace in Phyladel

CHAPTER I
The Cliffs of Splendohr

*I*t's just too good to last, thought soon-to-be nine-year-old Wesley. It was just a couple of days before the birthday party King Reagale had been planning for the boy. While it was a very special day, and one worthy of great celebration, the day wasn't Wesley's actual birthday in the traditional sense of the word. It was the celebration of Wesley coming to the kingdom of Orza one year prior, after the king had rescued the boy from his captivity. It was really at that point that young Wesley would say his life had truly begun, and the king wanted to commemorate the important event in royal fashion.

When Reagale, king of Orza, rescued him from the Trenzanian capital of Empiressen nearly three hundred and sixty-five days earlier, Wesley was a street urchin, a beggar—completely destitute. Reagale had traded him life for death and had brought him into his home as his own son. While the adoption itself was not yet finalized, papers were being drawn up even now, and all in the kingdom knew the king's intent to make Wesley his son and heir.

It had been a wonderful year, far better than any time in the young boy's previous life in Empiressen. Although he still missed his mother horribly, whom he presumed to be dead at the hands of the mercenaries in the dungeons of Prince Darius of Trenza, Wesley had found much joy in his new life with Reagale.

Things could not have been better in Wesley's life, yet he had an irrational, haunting feeling that something terrible was about to happen.

In the palace dungeon of the evil lord of Trenza, rumors were again being circulated among the prisoners that one day soon a deliverer would come to set the captives free. This rumor seemed to come back to life again with every passing generation of prisoners as they tried desperately to hold on to some hope of escape from the horrible existence that they knew day after day after horrible day. They knew that, apart from being rescued, they would probably endure this torture and drudgery until the day they died.

But who would be the one, this 'rescuer'? Would he be one of their own, or come from the outside? Someone from Empiressen, or from one of the other Trenzanian provinces? No one ever dreamed that he might actually come from Orza. He would certainly have to be a great warrior and incredibly strong. And he would have to have a large band of men under his command in order to overtake the many guards stationed around the castle and dungeon, not to mention the army of thugs Darius kept on a leash to do his bidding. Well, for now, they would leave the details out of the picture and just remain hopeful; for this faint glimmer of hope, as unlikely as it seemed, was all they had to hold on to.

Now, in one of the dungeon's main chambers, slumped in a dark corner in a feeble attempt at sleep, lay what was once a beautiful, enchanting young lady. Now a pitiful figure, the woman lay thin and pale. Her clothing, once at least tended and presentable, now hung from her fragile frame tattered, dirty and filled with holes from the harsh treatment of her imprisonment. Her blond hair hung in matted tangles from the crown of her head. The one who had once labored so hard in the fields now lay a weak, crumpled heap on the cold stone floor. The arms that had once caressed her child now lay limp and lifeless. Her pale blue eyes were washed continually by tears of despair, fear and worry. Her name was Gabriella of Trent.

Gabriella thought about her son day and night, hoping beyond hope that somehow he was all right, although she knew that the streets of Empiressen did not take kindly to little beggar children. She hoped that maybe someone had found pity in their heart and taken the boy in to care for him. But her heart sank as she thought of the improbability of that happening, especially in a city where so few cared about anything but themselves and meeting their difficult labor requirements for the prince. It was hard enough for the townspeople to gather sufficient crops to appease Darius and hopefully enough to feed their *own* children without taking in a homeless beggar. Fear gripped her heart as she imagined Wesley on a street corner pleading for bread, but finding none to help. The reality hit her unmercifully. She would probably never see her son again. It was enough to lose the husband whom she loved so dearly, but now to be separated from her only son, one so sweet and tender and innocent, one so young and helpless, one so fragile and in need of protection, one so in need of his mother to care for him, was more than her aching heart could bear. Anguish swept over her with a crushing weight. The mother wept bitterly for her little child.

*****

When they weren't walking and talking in the garden, sometimes the king and the boy would go around behind their palace, Calla Alesse, and skip stones in the large lily-dotted pond there. Other times they would go horseback riding together through the rolling green hills of the countryside. Up the heather-covered hills, down into the lush valleys, through the wooded highlands, beside the wet, marshy bog lands, splashing through bubbling, laughing brooks and over moss-covered stones, galloping in the open meadows, the two horses would bound.

The king rode a milky white stallion named "Silver." Wesley rode a chocolate brown pony with a caramel-colored mane (only no one told him it was only a pony and not a full-fledged horse).

3

Wesley was given the honor of naming his pony. He chose the name "Nibbles" because it seemed like he always wanted to stop and eat the clover in the fields.

Wesley delighted in taking these scenic tours of the breath-taking countryside. There was such a diversity of landscape. Also, the fertility of the earth here made for a vast variety of plant life. Unlike the useless, sandy soil in so many parts of Trenza, this soil was a rich, deep brown—the kind of soil that nothing can *help* but grow in.

One morning King Reagale called for Wesley quite a bit earlier than usual. In fact, the sun had not yet risen in the sky. Wesley rubbed the sleep from his eyes and gave a big stretch.

"I have some special plans for this morning, little one. There is something I want to show you." They walked down through the wet, dewy grass to the stables and saddled up Nibbles and Silver. The horses were rather sleepy, too, but quickly got caught up in the excitement of their riders. The king took the lead, Wesley trotting close behind. Navigating was tricky because it was still a bit difficult to see where one was going. But he had learned well enough by now that as long as he walked in the footsteps of the king, or in this case rode in the hoof prints of the king, he was in the best possible place he could be.

Down the steep hill from the castle they rode, and over the sunny southeastern slopes (which were not too sunny at this hour of the morning!), descending into the Valley of Nobb. From there they continued on between the twin hills (which Wesley insisted on calling 'camel humps,' because that's what they looked like to him), and through the orchards and grassy glens of Ballyn. It was getting a little easier to see now, as the sun was approaching the horizon, and they were able to pick up their pace a bit. Soon they came into an open, flat meadow. A gentle breeze was sending rippling waves through the sea of tall grasses.

The clearing ended abruptly at a sheer cliff, which looked down on miles of beach below. They had finally reached the Cliffs of Splendohr. Wesley had heard talk of this place but had never ventured this far into the countryside. The vast ocean lay stretched out before them as far as the eye could see, painted a lovely pale pink with the reflection of the sky. The king stopped several yards away from the precipice. Wesley stopped alongside of him, giving a little shudder and drawing his cloak around him a bit tighter, as there was still quite a chill in the air, especially now that they were nearer the water. By this time the horses were panting hard and were very glad for the much-needed break.

Reagale dismounted first, the young lad following quickly after. Tying their horses to a couple of nearby white birches, they then walked over a bit closer to the cliff's jagged edge.

"Do you think we might get a glimpse of Murkannos?" asked the boy excitedly.

"No, dear one. The sea monster dwells on the north side of Orza, in the Amarine Ocean. This is the South Sea."

Wesley nodded sheepishly, a bit ashamed of his apparent lack of geographical knowledge.

"I brought you here to give you a glimpse of the future, son—your future," whispered the lord of Orza, almost as if speaking any louder would break some magic spell that was at work. Wesley looked curiously at the nobleman.

"You see, Wesley, as wonderful as Orza is, it is merely a prelude to a life so fantastically wonderful that it staggers the imagination; a dim reflection of a place so glorious that you'll never be able to comprehend it on this side of its jeweled gates."

"Altierra, right?" asked the boy excitedly.

5

"Yes, dear, Altierra. No eye has ever seen, nor ear heard, nor mind ever conceived the things which I am preparing for you there, and for all of the others who love me."

The king looked out over the vast expanse of water which lay before them.

"What do you see?" he asked the boy.

"I see a great sea, My Lord," said Wesley.

"Keep watching off into the distance, Son of Trenza, where the water meets the sky and you will see the kingdom to come, the vast, glorious empire of my father." Then the king stooped down and gently touched the boy's eyes with the fingers of his right hand. He quietly breathed the words, "Father, please give this little one eyes to see your great and magnificent kingdom." When he removed his hand he said, "Now what do you see?"

"Why...why... I see a mountain toward the horizon a very far distance away, a great mountain looming out of the midst of the ocean... Oh, and now I see a range of smaller mountains all around it on every side. It is majestic and beautiful"...*and very, very mysterious*, thought Wesley. He could see a misty haze all around the top of the highest mountain and every once in a while he could see a sharp, forked flash of lightning in the midst of the clouds about its peak.

"That, my son, is Altierra—the City of Life. To this kingdom I must return one day in order to help my father finish the construction of this glorious land."

These words perplexed Wesley as much now as when Reagale had first broached the subject in the garden just days before. The thought had never occurred to Wesley that there could be a place even greater and more wonderful than this land of Orza which he now called home. Was he to set his eyes on yet another land as his final destination? What could this all mean? He still did not understand it all.

"But, why could I not see it before, when we first arrived here?" questioned the boy, inquisitively.

"Because you had need of me to give you the eyes to see. No one can see this great wonder unless I open their eyes to see it." The king paused thoughtfully for a moment. "When I go to Altierra I will prepare a place there for you so that you can come as well and be with me forever. But until then, I have much to prepare you for, my son. There are still evil forces at work who would like to see you, as my heir, destroyed. But don't be afraid, for although one day I will go away and you will not see me for a while, I will be with you always. And if you will learn well now and heed my words and my training, you will be victorious over all of the enemies of Liam."

A shadow passed over Wesley's face. The boy looked down to the ground.

"When are you going away?" His voice reflected the sadness of his heart. "I don't want you to leave. Please, don't leave mc."

The king reached down and picked up the youngster, wrapped his muscular arms around him, and held him tight.

"I will return to get you as soon as possible, dear heart, and then I promise that we shall never, never again be apart. But I won't be leaving for some time yet, as I still have much to do here in Orza before I go. So don't fret." He gave Wesley a little tickle under his arm, and the two shared a moment of laughter.

Then, out of the corner of his eye, Wesley noticed that something was beginning to happen on the eastern horizon. The sun was just now beginning to peek over the water's edge, its half-circle shape framing the glorious mountain of Altierra with a background of bright red-orange fire. What followed was a dazzling display of light. As the sun rose higher in the sky it began to reflect off the majestic city, with all its precious stones and glimmering gold. The sky virtually exploded in a radiant show of color and light, and a brilliant seven-pointed star appeared over the water and remained there for several minutes. The two stood there and watched for what seemed an eternity (really it was only ten minutes, but ten minutes seems like forever to an eight-year-old).

Wesley rubbed his eyes, straining to see more clearly. Then a distant noise caught his attention. It sounded like the rumbling of an earthquake or similar to the sound that tornadoes would make as they ravaged through the farmlands of his former home. As he listened, it was growing louder and louder and louder. Wesley put his hands over his ears to muffle the deafening noise.

All of a sudden, before he knew what was happening, Wesley found himself being swept up off the ground by a very forceful current of air that had funneled up from the bottom of the cliff with tornado-like force. The gust of air whisked the lad right off of the cliff's jagged edge!

CHAPTER II
The Journey of Promise

T hrough the air he tumbled, being hurled onward toward the bright light, faster and faster. It was as if some great hands were carrying him to the land beyond the sea. Strangely enough, though, he still felt the loving arms of the king holding him ever so tightly, unwilling to let him go. Wesley was amazed that he did not feel the least bit afraid, partly because he knew the king was still with him. Just knowing that made him feel safe.

On and on they flew, on and on... Wesley decided to close his eyes for a while, not because he was afraid, but because he was getting quite dizzy from tumbling and spinning and watching things whiz by at such a rapid pace. He was startled by a sudden, but gentle *thump* as they landed, and then...stillness. Wesley slowly opened up his eyes. What he saw at that moment was nothing short of incredible—so much so that he really believed that he must have somehow fallen asleep and was just dreaming a wonderful dream, the best one ever. But this was really even too glorious to be a dream.

"*Now* what do you see," said the king, a broad smile spreading over his bearded face. Wesley, still held tightly in the king's arms, simply looked up into Reagale's face, mouth ajar—or, I should say, downright *gaping*. Rendered utterly speechless by his new surroundings, more beautiful than he could have ever imagined, the boy looked one way, then the next, trying to grasp and take in all that he saw in this place.

When he finally got his wits about him, he whispered, "Where are we?"

"Altierra, my son. We are in Altierra. I wanted to give you a taste of what is to come that would engrave itself in your mind and implant itself in your heart. I wanted you to see the land to which I will be going, the land in which you will come and live with me one day. In the times ahead after my departure, this memory will be one that will carry and sustain you, and will give you hope for the future. Come, let me show you around a bit."

Now, dear reader, I must pause from my tale for a moment, as I am sure that you wish me to describe this great city in which our characters have found themselves in fine detail from earth to sky. But I could no sooner do that than give you the moon, for I would surely do an utter injustice to the place altogether. I will, however, make a feeble attempt to paint somewhat of a portrait, although a dim reflection of reality, in order to attempt to satisfy and placate your curiosity.

Imagine for a moment the beauty of fields where the silken tassels of dark green corn husks and heads of golden wheat wave gently in the breeze. Or picture in your mind vast, beautifully sculptured gardens where magnolias bloom, roses spill out their sweet perfume, and pansies lift their faces toward the sun. Think of a place where giant purple mountains with white caps rise so high that they meet with the sky above. Think of a place where valleys run deep and lush, with every kind of living thing running wild and free and enjoying a peaceful existence with one another. Imagine a land where the air itself is filled with song and joy fills the hearts of all who hear it, and they cannot help themselves from singing along and dancing to its enchanted melody. Imagine a place where great and magnificent canyons have been forged out, with deep blue rivers running through their fertile ravines.

Contemplate a city whose streets are entirely laid with gold and inset with precious jewels, just to be trampled underfoot by its inhabitants, and whose fortified gates are solid diamond with posts of ruby and pearl. Picture a world where all you have to do is *think* you want something, and it is in your hand the very next moment, or where all you have to do is *contemplate* about some place you want to be, and you are there already. Meditate on the thought of a place where work is as play and you tire not, no matter how long you labor. Ponder a place where all your dreams, your heart's innermost desires and longings, your wildest and most creative thoughts, whims and ideas are perfectly fulfilled; a place where your talents are so magnified that you are a master at whatever you set your hands to do. Consider a place where there are no enemies, no wars, and no hatred...just peace. Imagine a place where love reigns and sorrow and tears are no more, where joy abounds and pain and death have ceased to be. That is *Altierra* – The City of Life.

The two adventurers found themselves in the midst of a vast, open countryside. Crocuses, poppies, pansies, primroses and many other varieties of wildflowers that Wesley had never seen before blanketed the meadow with an exhilarating rainbow of color. Wesley thought the colors here were at least one thousand times deeper and richer than even the most lovely ones back in Orza. The fragrance of all these flowers rose up and engulfed him, overwhelming his senses and enhancing the beauty of these delicate creations all the more. He had never smelled such a sweet, satisfying aroma. The flower-rich, hilly landscape was dotted in each direction with several large castle-like structures, and marked off like a patchwork quilt with what looked to Wesley to be glistening, golden streams of water reflecting back the sun's light.

"There sure is a lot of water here," said Wesley, squinting as he looked at one of them.

"Water?" the king looked puzzled.

"Yes, all those golden rivers all over the place." Wesley pointed to one of the glowing streams.

"Oh!" said Reagale. "They are not rivers of gold; they are *streets* of gold."

"Like gold that you can walk on?" Wesley's eyes became as big as saucers.

"Yes, dear, like gold that you can walk on," laughed the king. "Let's take a little walk around." They hadn't gone far when the child posed another question.

"How many kings are there in this land, Father?" This was one of the very first times he had called Reagale 'Father.' He liked the way it sounded. He liked the way it felt.

"Only one king, my child. My father and I serve as one throne, rather than as two separate sovereigns. But, why do you ask?"

"Well, why are there so many castles, then?" inquired Wesley, pointing to the many large structures which dotted the hilly countryside.

"They are not really castles, but the mansions my father and I are preparing for all those who will come here to dwell in the land with us." Wesley's eyes grew big once more.

"Will *I* have a mansion someday?" he asked excitedly.

"As surely as I live and breathe, child," chuckled the monarch. "That is why I have to return here. I have to prepare a place for you, and for many others, too. There is much work yet to be done."

"I am going to miss you something awful when you go, but I sure am excited that you are coming here to make me a castle!"

"Mansion," corrected the grinning dignitary. Wesley looked around where they were now standing. There was a cluster of trees just off to their right with branches spaced out just right for an eight-year-old to climb, thought Wesley. There was an embankment just beyond them that sloped gently down a bit, and at its base was a babbling brook dancing playfully. He thought how he would love to skip some stones across the sparkling stream. Several large rocks made a pathway to the grassy bank on the other side.

Wesley noticed that there were wooden stakes and ropes marking off a very large section of the open field nearby. Assuming that they were the markings for the foundation of one of the mansions, he asked, "Who gets to live in this one when it is done?"

"You do," said the king. "That is, if you like this location well enough."

"If I *like* it?!!" he exclaimed. The youngster leapt into the air with a whoop and a shout of delight. "It's *perfect*! I couldn't have picked a more perfect one. I *love* it!"

"I knew you would!" said the king with delight. "When I return here, yours is the first to be built... promise!"

"*Ohhhh!*" The boy's face lit up and he threw his arms around Reagale, giving him the tightest hug he could muster and an emphatic kiss on the cheek.

Wheeeewwwwwwww...Wheeeewwwwwww...

The wind was beginning to pick up again.

"Hold on tight, Wesley. It is time for us to return from here...for now." He flashed the youngster a smile. The boy tightened his grip and buried his head in his royal escort's cloak. A gust from behind lifted the two airborne once more.

"Whoa, I'm getting dizzy again," giggled Wesley, as they spun around in the air and proceeded back the way they had come.

In but a few moments their feet were firmly planted on Orza's soil once more. Wesley loosened his hold on the king and slipped to the ground. He turned for one last look out across the sea. He was amazed at how still the water on the ocean was, like a sea of glass. It was as if the great wind had not stirred it at all. The sun, now risen halfway in the sky, revealed that they had been gone for several hours; but, surprisingly enough, it seemed like only minutes.

They turned to untie Silver and Nibbles, a reverent hush filling the air as if they stood on holy ground. Wesley's heart felt so full and satisfied. He was running over and over in his mind the many events of the morning, anxiously trying not to forget any tiny detail, any sight or color he had seen, any words that he and the king had exchanged, any feelings that he had felt. He never wanted to forget. Almost as if he knew what Wesley was thinking, the king said, "Write it down, lad. Write it all down so that you, and all those who read it, may live with hope."

Wesley nodded in agreement. That was all that either spoke on the ride back home, for words would have ruined the magic that still lingered in the air.

CHAPTER III
Adventure at the Beach and the Birthday Bash

In the months that followed, they reminisced often about their shared experience on the cliffs that day. A couple of times Wesley had even ventured back there on his own, in hopes of reliving the adventure. He would stand on the edge of the cliff (but not too close!), lift his face to the sky, shut his eyes, and wait... and wait... and wait... but in the end he left with only the memories, and memoirs, of his first exploit with King Reagale.

One fine summer morning while the dew still lay on the grass, Wesley embarked on one of these hopeful trips. As any young boy, Wesley loved an adventure. And this day would prove to be an adventure of the most wonderful kind. He had ransacked the pantry and cold-room of the castle's kitchen before he departed, and filled his sack with leftovers from dinner the night before. He figured he would ride to the cliffs and have himself a little picnic.

But, after he arrived at the precipice, he made a delightful discovery that changed the entire course of his day. Quite hidden by the low-hanging branches of several trees, he found the entrance to a narrow, winding path on the right-hand side of the cliff. Once he broke off the obstructing limbs, he found that it was just wide enough for his horse to manage. It was slow going because it was very steep, and as a result of all the brush which had grown in upon the path. Wesley held his arm out in front of his face to fend off an occasional bough from hitting him square on.

At last they reached the bottom and came out into a clearing. What a hidden treasure they had found — a private cove with a nice, big beach! They ventured out into the open to survey their

15

findings. Wesley glanced up to the Cliffs of Splendohr, which were now towering high above him, and he thought how very small he felt all of a sudden. On either side of the cove were crags and rocks. He even saw a couple of cave openings, which he took note of for future expeditions.

Mid-morning now, it was proving to be a lovely, sunny day, and quite warm. The white sand contrasted sharply with the teal blue water of the sea. Wesley, holding tightly to the horn of his saddle, swung his leg around and dismounted from his pony, feet sinking several inches into the cool, spongy sand. Deciding that it would be best to keep Nibbles here in the shade, he tied his reigns to a nearby birch tree. He peeled off his sweat-soaked shirt, then looked around until he found a small, grassy patch to sit down on and unfasten his sandals (because it is altogether very uncomfortable to have to get back on your horse and ride any distance with togs full of sand).

Wesley stood up and drew in a long, deep breath. Some said the seashore smelled like dead fish, especially in the marshy areas. But Wesley loved the smell of the sea. A couple of playful gulls swooped low overhead with a friendly greeting of "**caw, caw, caw, cawww.**" Wesley thought he would have a little fun with them. He closed his fist, and then moved his arm up and down, giving the impression that he had a choice morsel to throw up for the two hungry birds. They hovered around above the boy, waiting with great anticipation. Wesley threw his arm up in the air one last time and opened his hand, releasing the imaginary food.

The gulls went into a frenzy, circling and swooping, trying to find whatever it was that Wesley had thrown, but to no avail. After several seconds of this they looked back at the boy and cocked their heads to the side in a puzzled sort of way, then flew off. Wesley was laughing so hard at this point that he was doubled over, clutching his stomach. When he finally recovered from laughing at his joke, he decided a little swim would be a splendid idea.

He stepped over several pieces of randomly strewn driftwood lying here and there, and proceeded to the water's edge. The small waves curled and lapped at the soft sand. Wesley stepped gingerly into the water, testing it first with the tips of his toes to see how cold it was. *Ahhhh, just right!* He looked out over the great expanse of ocean before him. He thought it fascinating that the waves started out so big farther from the shore, and then kept getting smaller and smaller until they just rolled in gracefully and licked gently at his feet. He waded out into the cool, refreshing salt water, cautiously avoiding a few broken shells and pieces of coral as he went.

Wesley enjoyed the feeling he got by letting the waves lift and then drop him in their folly as they headed toward the shore. He could feel the powder-fine sand slipping away from beneath his feet as the undercurrent swept back out toward the open sea. The water was so clear that Wesley could see the whole way down to the bottom, even when the water was up to his shoulders. He could even see some fish swim by occasionally, usually small ones this close to the shore, but most of them were very brightly colored and spectacular to look at.

The boy frolicked for a long time in the crystal clear water, only coming out for a brief moment to grab a quick bite of the food he had packed, then getting right back in to play again. When his skin began to prune up and he felt his teeth chattering, he decided it *might* be time to get out. He waded back to shore and up onto the warm sand of the beach. Unfortunately, because he had not planned to go swimming, he had not brought a towel. He would just have to lie on the sand and let the sun warm him up and bake him dry. He gave a good shake to get off as much excess water as he could, much the way a wet dog does, and then looked for a sunny spot to lie in.

17

He lay down (forgetting that he would now have a frightfully scratchy ride home) and tried to get comfortable. He felt something just below the surface of the sand sticking irritatingly into his back. He rolled over, dug the item up and blew the sand off. To his delight, he saw that it was a beautifully formed conch shell. It was white, with beige, brown and caramel-colored swirls. And what was amazing about it was that there was another almost identical, yet smaller, conch shell fit perfectly inside of the larger one. *What luck!* thought Wesley. He studied the two shells more. *They remind me, in a way, of the King and me,* he thought. *A perfect fit!* He took his prize over and placed it in the pouch of the horse's saddle bag, just another little hidden treasure along the way. The boy went back to lie down in the warmth of the sun, and fell fast asleep.

When Wesley awoke, he realized that the sun was now quite a bit farther down in the sky. Wesley guessed that it was somewhere between three and four in the afternoon, and he should probably be heading back soon. He was also very hungry after all this salt air and he *definitely* didn't want to be late for dinner tonight! He put his shirt back on and prepared to leave. *One more thing I have to do,* he thought. He went over to Nibbles, untied his reins and walked him to the water's edge. He decided it would be good to get his horse nice and cooled off before the long ride home.

Wesley mounted his faithful steed, and then rode him out several feet into the cool water. Wesley pulled the pony's reins to face him southward, gave him a little kick in the side and a loud "Hyyyahhhh!" and off they went like a shot. He galloped Nibbles along the coast of the crystal blue-green sea, soaking them both thoroughly as the water kicked up in a flurry from the horse's hooves. *This is great sport,* thought Wesley, *although I probably should have thought to do it* before *I dried off!* He raced back and forth along the shoreline a couple more times. Wesley laughed aloud when he thought about how he must look by now – quite like a drowned rat, to be sure!

Wesley thought he saw something out of the corner of his eye. He looked out toward the sea. There on the horizon he *saw* it – *Altierra!* There it was in all its enormity, in all its splendor, just as he had seen it that famed day with the king. Some salt water dripped from his soaking wet hair into his eyes. He rubbed them to get it out and clear his blurred vision. He looked out again. It was gone.

*****

"Father, Father! I saw it, I saw it, I saw – "

"Whoa, slow down there, lad," the king laughed at the sight of the disheveled, stiff-haired boy running toward him. Wesley did look pretty funny. The combination of salt water and sand mixed in throughout his hair, and the fact that he had raced back so fast that the wind had dried it sticking straight up on end, was a comical sight for anyone to behold. Reagale drew Wesley near and gave him a big hug.

"Now then, take a deep breath and tell me all about what you did and what you saw, son." So Wesley related all the adventures of the day: the hidden cove, the refreshing swim, the two conch shells he found, racing his pony in the water, and seeing Altierra.

"Wesley, can I see the two shells you found?" asked the king. Wesley had taken them from the saddle bag and placed them in his pants pocket. He pulled them out and handed them to Reagale.

"Hmmmm..." said the king with a knowing grin. "They remind me, in a way, of you and me – a perfect fit!"

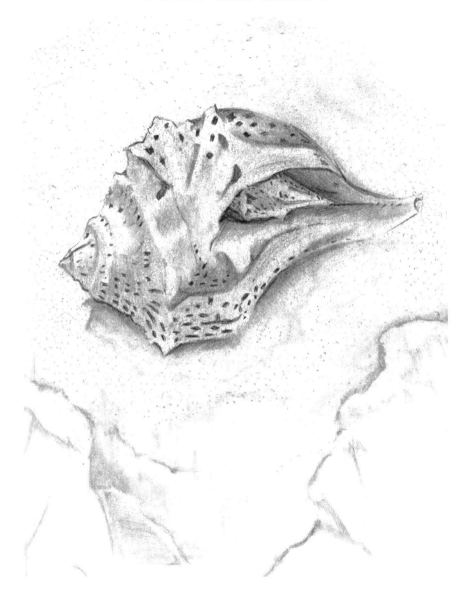

The stiff-haired boy's mouth fell open at Reagale's words, and the king let out a roaring laugh as he pulled the stunned boy close and gave him one of his best bear hugs, spinning him around a couple of times for good measure. Oh, how he loved this child.

*****

The moments they shared together had turned to days, and the days had turned to weeks, and the weeks had turned to months. Before they knew it, it had been one full year since the king had rescued the boy from his captivity. It almost seemed a dream now, Wesley's former life. It was as if this, in only 1 year, was the only life he had ever known. Except for the memory of his parents, his prior history in Trenza was black, empty and lifeless. Before this, all seemed to him a dim shadow or mere reflection of this new life he had been given. And why him? He still found himself perplexed by this gnawing question. He knew it was nothing he had done to earn or deserve this favor, this great grace which had so freely been bestowed upon him. It was just the kindness, generosity and loving heart of the king.

There was only one thing missing—his mother. How he longed for her to be with him, if she was even still alive. He thought about her often, even now. She would have been so happy for him.

The day of Wesley's party finally arrived. Almost all the people in the city descended upon the palace that evening for the happy occasion. Citizens of Phyladel, young and old and those in between, noblemen and noblewomen, farmers and merchants, all dressed in their finest attire and with their dancing shoes on (for, if there's one thing Orzanians LOVE, it's to dance!).

The king stood with his young guest of honor at the front entrance to the castle, warmly greeting and welcoming all as they entered. Wesley was a bit embarrassed that all of this fuss was just for him.

It was simply a delightful evening. The king had arranged for a grand feast in the massive main banquet hall. There were many tables spread with every good thing to eat and drink that you could possibly imagine. As everyone ate, the king made a short speech. He recounted the story of how he had found Wesley and of their adventurous journey back to Orza. The king finished by bringing Wesley to the front. He knelt on one knee and reminded Wesley, in the presence of all, of the covenant he had made to him the year before.

"I give you my word as king that I will provide for all of your needs according to the great riches of the storehouses of my kingdom and that you will never again know want. I give you my word as king that I will seek to do you good and not evil all the days of your life, and I promise to look after and protect you. I will give you a good future, one filled with hope. I love you, son."

These words seemed as incredible to Wesley now as they had when the king had uttered them the very first time. Wesley flung his arms around the ruler's neck. There wasn't a dry eye in the entire ballroom, including Wesley's and the king's.

After everyone had their fill, the dishes and all the tables were removed, the floor was cleared, and the king's minstrels came out and began to play. Their merry tunes rang out through the banquet hall and down each corridor of the palace. The songs they played were joyful, with a fast tempo and a happy melody. The floor was quickly filled again, this time not with tables, but with many delighted foot-stomping partygoers, kicking up their heels in celebration. Wesley couldn't remember ever having a more wonderful time. Life was good—indeed, life was *very* good, but all that was about to change.

CHAPTER IV
Treachery, Treason and Terror

$\mathfrak{T}$he evening continued on and on, as if there would be no end. Evening flowed into night, and still there were no signs of the festivities stopping. No one seemed to tire of the merrymaking — not the dancers, not the minstrels, not Reagale, and *certainly* not Wesley! The excited boy bounded up the short flight of marble steps to the landing where the dignitary was standing looking out over the main floor of the ballroom, enjoying watching the revelry.

"Psst..," he beckoned with his finger for Reagale to bend down a bit more to his level. The king bent over and Wesley again threw his arms enthusiastically around his neck, very nearly knocking the unsuspecting king off balance.

"Thank you *soooo* much for the birthday party! I have never had such a good time in all my life. Thank you!" He gave the king a big, chocolate-covered kiss on the cheek.

Just then there was a great thud as the huge, heavy, metal doors at the back of the large room swung open with a great force. A chilling wind swept through the room, causing the many candles lit throughout to flicker, and sending shivers up Wesley's spine.

Every eye in the room turned toward the entryway. A dark, sinister figure emerged from the shadows of the hallway. There in the doorway stood a tall man, enrobed in an oversized black cloak, face shadowed by the large hood which covered his head. Behind him appeared six figures, all dressed in similar fashion.

"What is your business here?" asked the king calmly, with unshaken boldness and authority. The unexpected visitor in the front removed the black hood which hid his face, revealing none other than the dreaded lord of Trenza himself!

"We have come to request an audience with Your Majesty," hissed Darius.

"Your timing is less than appropriate. Nevertheless, you may approach."

The evil prince entered the ballroom bowing low, his still-hooded entourage following close behind. Even Darius recognized the dominion and authority of King Reagale Constance, although he hated everything about Reagale and everything that he represented.

"Your Highness," he spat with disdain, "I have a legal matter I wish to resolve with you."

"What matter would that be, Darius?" returned the king unflinchingly.

Darius reached beneath his cloak and pulled out a rolled parchment. He undid the tie, and then opened the paper. "You are, I am confident, aware of the law of the ancients which states that, and I quote,

> *Any person who is caught in thievery will become slave to him from whom he has stolen property and/or goods, and his life may be required of him depending upon the wishes of the person from whom he stole and the value of the property and/or goods stolen from said individual.*

"I am aware of this law, Darius. How does this concern me and my kingdom?"

Darius motioned for one of his six escorts to step forward. The mysterious hooded figure obeyed. As he pushed back the hood of his black cloak, gasps went up from the court. To their shock and dismay, there stood Mari, one of the tenders of King Reagale's palace gardens.

"So, now we know where you have disappeared to this week, my friend," said the king, obvious disappointment in his voice. "How could you betray the one who loved you as his own? The betrayal of a trusted friend is truly the most bitter indeed."

Mari stood seemingly unmoved and unrepentant, face stern with resolve to complete his task. "Mari, reveal the item we hold as evidence!" came the command. Mari reached beneath his cloak and took out something polished and shiny.

"My cup!" cried Wesley. Prickles went up his spine and his face became a heated flush. He felt his insides knot up with fear.

"Actually, this is *my* cup," hissed the evil lord, taking the cup and walking slowly toward the boy. "You will notice my initials engraved on the side, *ſD* for Lord Darius. I sent the item out with a number of other precious artifacts to be cleaned and have the tarnish removed. And now, my faithful servant," he said, looking at Mari, "why don't you tell the king where you uncovered my missing cup."

"I found it in the boy's bedroom in the bottom of his chest," declared Mari smugly, pointing a thin, bony finger in accusation at the blushing child.

"*Ohhhhh,*" hushed cries and concerned whispers could be heard echoing throughout the great hall.

"This chalice is solid silver and is a priceless part of my royal treasury. I demand that the little thief be turned over to me to do with as I see fit, for there must be justice and severe punishment fitting for this crime!"

Wesley had never before seen the king angry, but now his eyes blazed with a fire of holy wrath. The ruler was outraged at the accusations being hurled against the one he loved so dearly.

"Ask him for yourself, Sire, if these allegations be true or false," said the wicked prince, again bowing low to the ground and trembling in fear at the king's show of rage.

Reagale brought the boy to his side and drew him close. "My dear Wesley, have you done such a thing as you are accused of?"

The boy hung his head in shame. "Yes, My Lord, I have done as he said. It was a couple of weeks after my mother was taken. I took the cup from someone I thought to be a traveling vendor. I...I didn't know that he worked for Lord Darius. I needed a cup to beg with, and I had no money, so...so... I stole the cup," he stammered.

"There! You have heard it with your own ears!" Darius interjected. "There is no denying the charges. Turn the boy over to me and we will be on our way. He will either live as my slave or he will die. That is for *me* to decide!" declared the accuser venomously.

Now, in the kingdoms of Orza and Trenza, a man might decide to adopt a child, and may even share his intentions with family and friends. However, there was paperwork to fill out and a special ceremony that needed to take place in the public arena before the adoption could be official and legally binding. In this

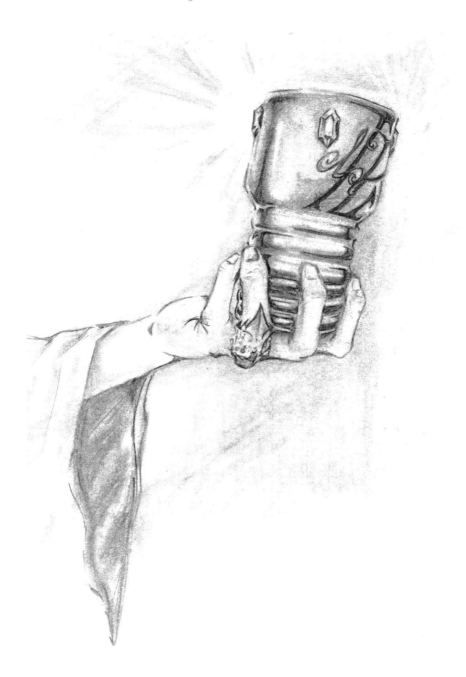

ceremony, the child would be brought before the constituted authorities, papers would be signed, his or her former garments would be removed, and the proposed father would give the child clothing suitable to his or her new condition of life. Although the king already considered Wesley his son, his adoption had not yet been made public, legal and binding. Reagale knew that he could not legally stop Darius from taking the boy. The crime must be paid for, and Wesley did not yet have the protection of the status of being an official, legal member of the royal household. Because a legitimate law had been broken, he could not protect the child from the consequences of his actions. Wesley was, in essence, still under the prince's law and jurisdiction.

The king spoke softly, "My dear child, the prince is right that the penalty for the theft which you have committed is a life of servitude to the one stolen from...or death."

The boy began trembling in fear, and his face went a sickly, ashen color as he looked at the evil prince's face, with its twisted, sinister grin of triumph. His knees grew weak, and tears began to trickle down his round little cheeks. He had been thinking that all of this was too good to be true, too good to last. Now he could see that he was right. He would now be forced to leave his new home in the palace, to leave this beautiful kingdom, and to once again feel the pains of hunger gnawing in his belly. He would never be able to go to Altierra. But, most bitter of all, he would have to leave this man, this king he had grown to love so deeply and had come to call 'Father.' He might even lose his life for what he had done, but that seemed to him better than living separated from the king. Oh, he couldn't bear it!

"Please have mercy! Please, please have mercy on me!" Wesley ran down the steps and fell on his face before the evil lord, crying out in pitiful sobs. But there was no mercy to be found in Darius, for his heart was as cold as stone, and as cruel as hatred itself.

28

But then, out of the corner of his stinging, tear-filled eyes, Wesley saw something fall to the floor, then something else after it. He turned his head to see the dignitary shedding himself of his royal robes, stripping himself of his outer kingly garments. The boy looked at Reagale questioningly. "Brianna," summoned the king. His loyal friend hurried to his side and he whispered something into her ear.

As Brianna listened, her jaw dropped slowly, a look of shock, horror and despair overtaking her usually joyful face. Whatever the ruler had told her had overwhelmed her with emotion, and she gave the king a very tearful hug. She released her hold on her friend and lord and gave him a nod of consent. "I will, My Lord. I promise I will take good care of him," she said with firm resolve, drying her tear-streaked cheeks with her hands.

Everyone in the room, including Wesley, was still trying to understand what was happening. The king beckoned for the shaking child to come to him. Reagale drew him up into his great arms and held him tightly. Wesley buried his head in the king's neck. "Wesley, do you remember the covenant I made to you?" Wesley shook his head to indicate that he did. "Even though what you did deserves punishment, for you have been unfaithful to the laws of the land, I cannot be unfaithful to the word of my covenant to you, for I cannot deny myself. Don't ever forget that what I do now I do because I love you so deeply. Whatever happens, you must not forget my love for you. For love conquers all evil." With that, Reagale placed the boy in Brianna's arms and whispered something to Kavin, the captain of the guard, who was now standing beside him.

Then the king turned to address the dark lord and said, "It is a truth that the penalty must be served." He held out his hands. "Take me instead of the boy." There were several gasps, and then the large room became eerily silent. After a few moments Darius's look of utter surprise gave way to a sinister, wicked laugh that came up from deep inside of him and echoed throughout every hallway and room in the palace. He looked deeply and triumphantly into the eyes of his prey and slowly and deliberately, with an heir of immense satisfaction, said simply, "Seize him."

The guards of the evil one looked at each other hesitantly. They were well aware of the power of this one they were just ordered to arrest. Four of them proceeded slowly up the short flight of marble steps toward where Reagale stood. One brave man (or *foolish* may be more accurate) took the lead, gritted his teeth, and wrapped the shackles around the king's wrists. As soon as the other guards saw that nothing bad had happened to him, they rushed on Reagale. They threw him to the ground and shackled his feet, kicking and punching him just for the fun of it. Then they grabbed him by both arms and dragged him down the stairs. As the king passed by Mari, he looked deeply into the eyes of his betrayer. His eyes seemed to become swords that pierced to the very core of Mari's heart. The traitor, unnerved and cut-to-the-quick, cast his own eyes downward, unable to look upon his former employer, provider and friend. Reagale had so benevolently taken him in, clothed and fed him, given him employ at the castle and provided for his needs faithfully for several years now.

It wasn't supposed to turn out this way. They were just supposed to take the boy back -- that's all! Mari wrestled with the two opposing voices that warred within his head — one to justify his treachery, the other to condemn it.

They led Reagale out of the palace courts, crying, "Victory is ours this day! Orza is ours!"

"No, no! It's not fair! I did it, not Him!" screamed Wesley. "Please, let him go!"

The prince of wickedness turned slowly around as he heard Wesley's voice and faced the youngster. "Don't worry, *boy.* Once the king is out of the way, I'll be back to take care of *you* too!" he spat, mouth in a twisted grin, the penetrating look of his eyes burning holes through the lad with the fire of their hatred. He spun on his heels and hurriedly took the lead of the fateful procession. A couple of the guards roughly blindfolded the king and threw him over one of their horses, securing the shackles which bound him with ropes to various parts of the horse's saddle.

Mari approached his own steed and prepared to mount. Darius turned to him and said, "I have no further need of you." Mari stood stunned, speechless and confused. "I have no place for weakness in my ranks!" he spat. "Don't you think I knew your thoughts back in the palace — the *regret* you had for your part in this, the *sympathy* you felt for *HIM*?!" he said with disdain. "Yes, I saw the look of remorse in your eyes as he passed. You are soft and completely useless to me. I relieve you of your duties and your position," he said with a cold matter-of-factness and a wave of his hand. He motioned to two of his soldiers nearby, who commenced removing Mari's outer cloak and the uniform he wore beneath it. Half-naked, stripped of his position and his pride, Mari hung his head in shame. He looked up at Reagale once more, laying helplessly across the horse that was to bear him to the land of no return, suddenly very aware that he had just offered up to death the only one that had ever *truly* loved him.

"I'm sorry," he whispered. A sickening feeling began in the pit of his stomach and seemed to course through every part of his being.

No one ever saw Mari after that day. Some said he went back to Trenza on his own. Others said that he had killed himself, unable to live with the guilt of what he had done.

"To Trenza!" came the bellowing command, and the company of hardened soldiers mounted and set off quickly behind their evil leader. For a few moments there was the thunder of hooves, and the screaming whinnying of their horses — then silence.

"Kavin!" screamed Wesley hysterically, not aware that the captain of the guard was just a few feet behind him.

"I am here, Wesley. I am here." He laid his hand on the boy's shoulder.

"*Do* something... Save him, please save him! Why don't you do something to save him? They're going to *kill* him!" Wesley's voice was wild with uncontrollable fear.

"I know, child," Kavin dropped his head in defeat. "But, alas, the king gave me strict orders that we are under NO circumstances to interfere, no matter what happens. We *cannot* disobey his orders, as much as we desperately *want* to!" said Kavin exasperatedly.

Wesley looked up at the guard, "I *must* go with him, Kavin... I can't let him go alone and think I don't care about him and what is happening to him, and it being all my fault in the first place. Will you come with me, please?" he pleaded.

"We will *all* come with you, child. We may not be able to interfere, but that doesn't mean that we can't accompany him at a distance. And I will order all the troops to remain on full alert in the hopes that the king will change his mind and signal us to attack. We will wait with *readiness* for the command to strike. Yes, lad, we will *all* come with you." He slipped an arm around the boy's slumped shoulders. "But now, let us make *haste*, for it will take some time to assemble the troops, and we don't want them to have too much of a start on us. We haven't a moment to lose!"

As the rest of the army hurried to ready itself, arming themselves with various weapons of war and mounting their horses, Wesley ran down the hill to the stables. He threw open the barn door and darted through the stalls until he found his faithful pony. Nibbles vigorously shook his chocolate-colored mane in greeting. As Wesley saddled up his pony (quicker than he ever had before), the king's own horse, Silver, looked up at the boy inquisitively.

"Don't worry, boy. We'll get him back for you, if it's the last thing we do!" He mounted his horse and rode him swiftly back up the grassy slope to the courtyard in front of the palace where the troops were beginning to gather. It seemed as if even the pony could sense that something was terribly wrong. He kept snorting and shaking his head and mane uneasily and stomping his front left hoof on the ground. Even little Nibbles was ready for battle. They would all do whatever it took to free their king.

Once the troops were assembled, they set out for the city of Empiressen. Kavin reasoned that Darius was probably taking the king there. They ran their horses as fast and as hard as they possibly could. There was no talking, just silence, sadness and a very tangible fear in the wake of the day's events. They wondered what lay ahead of them as this day of horror would progress.

CHAPTER V
The Death of a Dream

As they raced onward, each place along the road seemed to hold such special memories for Wesley; each one brought back to his mind the precious times with the king on their journey in the opposite direction just one year before. The memories, under the circumstances, made Wesley's pain even more bitter.

All through the night they rode. They reached the gates of the city of Empiressen after about ten hours, much quicker than when Wesley had made this journey by foot with the king at his side so seemingly long ago. This was one place Wesley never thought he would ever see again—he had desperately hoped that he wouldn't, anyway.

It was early morning now, and a light drizzle was falling from the clouded sky. They quickly made their way through the tall iron gates, proceeded through the narrow city streets (which the boy remembered all too well), and headed straight for the dark castle which loomed in the distance. Wesley shuddered as they passed the fields where his mother and father had slaved. He could see the remains of their tiny cottage from the road even now. Wesley had a strange, hollow feeling inside—the kind you get sometimes when you have been away from someplace for a long while, someplace that was unpleasant, and then you suddenly find yourself back there and the memories come flooding back upon you with vengeance.

They were able to move through the city quickly because the streets were completely abandoned for some reason. There were vendors' carts left unattended with food still cooking on them, small curbside fires where people had been warming themselves left still burning, horses and plows left in the field as if to bring in the harvest themselves, yet not a soul anywhere to be seen. Even the houses they passed showed no signs of life. Where were all the townspeople?

The rain fell steady now. Flashes of forked lightning could be seen in the distance, but were growing brighter and closer. An occasional loud clap of thunder startled the horses. They finally reached the crest of the plateau at the far end of which the castle stood. There was a narrow strip of woods that encompassed the entire perimeter of the elevated stretch of land. They could see a great crowd assembled on the left-hand side of the large open plain, about halfway up the expansive field toward the dark lord's castle. One half of the troops, under Kavin's orders, veered to the right and quietly stole through the woods around the edge of the plateau so as to remain unseen. The other half of the troops, including Wesley and Kavin, veered left, also keeping to the woods for safety. A handful of men were ordered to stay behind with the horses. Within a few minutes, the entire woods surrounding the field was filled with the king's loyal subjects, the fire of battle in their eyes, swords drawn for what they hoped would become a rescue mission—waiting, just waiting for the king to give the orders and they would descend upon that place to rescue the one they loved. But no such order would ever come.

Kavin and Wesley, in an effort to see more clearly exactly what was taking place, found a thicket of evergreen bushes at the outskirts of the woods in which to crouch and hide, and were able to get surprisingly close to the assembly. What they saw there horrified them.

In the very center of the crowd rose a high gallows of wood. The lumber out of which it had been made appeared to be freshly hewn. By the look of it, the gallows seemed to have been constructed for this particular event.

The two hiding in the thicket strained to hear and see what was happening in the crowd, for there was an awful lot of commotion of some sort. Wesley decided to climb a nearby tree to get a better look.

A group of minstrels played a strange tune with an irregular rhythm. Some of the people were dancing wildly to the dissonant melody. A handful of villagers toward the outer edges of the gathering appeared to be weeping. Yet, at the same time, there was a larger number who could be heard mocking.

"O great king, take us back to your kingdom!" shouted one.

"We bow before your greatness, O omnipotent king!" taunted another.

"If you are such a great king why don't you save yourself? Hah!" they mocked.

"Where are all your loyal followers now?!" another chided boisterously, delivering one more staggering blow to Reagale's already disfigured face.

"*WE* ARE *HERE!!!*" shouted Wesley to himself. The boy climbed a little higher. He was high enough now that he could see down into the middle of the jeering crowd. He thought he recognized the faces of some of the villagers mingled in throughout the tumultuous gathering. And yes, now he could see *him*. There in the very center of the angry mob was his beloved king and father, wounded and bleeding terribly from the head and face.

Reagale was still blindfolded. Some men had emerged from the crowd of onlookers. They were beating him, kicking him, spitting in his face, pulling out his hair. Oh, Wesley could hardly bear to watch. *Please*, he thought, *give the order, give the order!* But the king remained silent. Wesley looked down from his perch and whispered loudly, "Kavin, I don't think he knows we are here!"

"Oh, child, he knows...he knows."

The jeering continued as the crowd pushed the nobleman closer and closer toward the waiting gallows. Prince Darius, face dark and shadowy, sneered with a sense of deep satisfaction. He was dressed in a black robe with a black hood over his head, which framed his hollowed cheeks and dark-circled eyes. He had by now ascended the stairway to the platform and declared himself judge, jury and executioner. He wanted to make this a show for all. He would kill the king of the land beyond, and would take over his kingdom, too — victory!

Two guards dragged the bound prisoner up the crude planked stairway to the waiting dictator. The wicked one approached Reagale as a snake ready to loose its venom on its prey. He reached up and ripped off Reagale's blindfold. "O great king," he mocked, "save yourself if you are so mighty! What's the matter? Cat got your tongue?!" He spat the words poisonously. "Now I have you and no one can save you from my hand!" He laughed sinisterly, delivered one last blow to the bloodied face of his silent victim, and then placed the course hemp rope around his neck. As Darius walked over and placed his hand on the release lever, there was a great stirring in the bushes and the trees on the outskirts of the field as those loyal to the lord of Orza poised themselves for attack. None of those assembled were aware of it, but the king could sense what was about to happen. He quickly held up his hand as a motion to his troops to stop them from taking any action on his behalf. Then Reagale looked up in the direction of the tree that had become Wesley's hiding spot, seemed to lock right in on the boy where he sat straddling a large branch (Wesley felt as if he was looking right into his eyes) and whispered a final, "*I love you.*" Somehow, even despite the distance, Wesley not only heard his father's words, but felt them penetrate deep into his heart.

Then, suddenly, Darius pulled the long wooden lever.
Crack, swish, thud! He erupted into a hideous, echoing laugh.
Wesley had turned his head away just in time to avoid seeing the
gruesome execution. He held his breath, afraid to even breathe.
He waited a few sickening seconds and then turned back to see his
rescuer dangling lifelessly at the end of the rope's tightened noose.

There was a great moan and gnashing of teeth from the
direction of the forest. Kavin stared in utter disbelief. He thought
for sure the king would summon them to battle on his behalf. *What
could his purpose have been for letting* this *happen, for allowing things to
go this far? Surely this will mean the end of all Orza, and the certain
conquest of our people. What was he thinking?! What good could
possibly come from this?* The great captain went limp. *If only he
would have let us help. We were here waiting, great in number, strong
enough to defeat and rescue. He knew we were here waiting to destroy his
enemies and rush to his aid. If only he would have given the command,* he
thought. Confused, overwhelmed and half numb, he fell to his
knees, head bowed low. His sword lay beside him, of no use now.
What was there left worth fighting for? All he had given his life to
was now gone, all he had lived for swept away in one devastating
moment. His king was dead. His eyes began to fill up as he
realized the gravity of what had just happened and the inevitable
consequences of this horrid event.

Wesley clamored recklessly down the tree and crumbled to
the muddy ground, tears flowing as freely as the rain, which, by
now, was a steady soaking. His little sobbing body heaved up and
down from the stabbing pain of his broken heart. Fear and pain
mingled together. To lose one father, then his mother, was pain a
little heart should never have to bear. To lose another father was
more than he felt he could ever endure. He lay on the cold, wet
earth, a crushed and broken, burdened, guilty thief who's crime
had caused the death of an innocent one, of a friend. Wesley was
faced with the cold, indisputable fact that everyone who had ever
loved him was gone and he was, once again, alone—an orphan.

"Let him hang there for a while as a public spectacle to all who pass by this way and to show everyone who is the *true* king, the greatest ruler in all the continent of Austire!" Darius shouted victoriously. "And, as it would seem, the *only* ruler now," he smiled with smug satisfaction.

The king's faithful troops waited until the vengeful crowd dispersed and everyone had gone. Then they stole silently out of the woods and made their way toward the towering instrument of death, from which their king still hung lifelessly.

Kavin ordered all of the troops to begin their journey back to Orza. "We will not be far behind you. I want to give the boy time to grieve, and we want to retrieve...his body..." Kavin choked back the emotion which flooded over him.

"As you wish, sir," came the solemn response.

Kavin and a few of his men carefully lifted the king down from the gallows and lay his still body on the wet ground, but not before a dozen or so of their company removed their cloaks and spread them beneath him. Oh, how they loved him. It all seemed so senseless.

Wesley pushed his way through the troops. Guilt flooded over him, knowing that the king died to pay the penalty for *his* wrong. He fell to his knees and lay sobbing over the broken, limp body. After several moments he lifted his head to look upon the one he loved. There were large beads of sweat upon his forehead, but they were tinged with red.

"Drops of sweat mixed with blood — the sign of a broken heart," stated Kavin, sadly. "Those with whom he had pleaded to return with him, those whom he had visited and desired with all his heart to help, they were the very ones who cried out for his murder, the very ones who tortured and killed him." He removed the handkerchief from his pocket and used it to wipe his master's brow.

Wesley touched the battered, bleeding face gently, as if he wanted to be careful not to cause the king any further pain. He bent down and kissed the cheek of the one who used to play with him, who laughed with him, who cared for him...who loved him. Wesley reflected over all the fun times they'd had, over all that the kindly king had done for him. He had reached down in the gutter and touched a dirty little untouchable boy whom no one else would touch, and had made him the son of a king. He had taken him from rags to riches and had given him a life that he could never have dreamed. And now he had given him life again, but it had meant his own death.

"It's my fault! It's all my fault!" he sobbed. Hopelessness and despair washed over his heart. He remembered experiencing these exact feelings before, when he lived in the streets as a beggar in this city. What irony that he would find himself back here again, overwhelmed with the exact same feelings and emotions. His world had gone black once more. He drew his cloak around him tighter. He was shivering from a combination of the steady falling rain, terror of the future without this man in it, fear for his very life now that his great protector was gone and complete anguish of soul at the loss of the best friend he had ever known and the one he had called 'Father.' When he could restrain himself no longer, he cried out in a heart-wrenching wail, buried his face in his small, dirt-smudged hands and wept inconsolably.

Several very solemn minutes passed. "Come, lad," said Kavin gently. "We can do no more good here. We must flee. We have to get away from here, for we are all in grave danger if we remain a moment longer. The guards may return soon or a passerby may alert the palace of our presence here." Kavin put a comforting arm around the boy's heaving shoulders and helped him to his feet. He led him in the direction of their horses, but Wesley couldn't take his eyes from the body of his lord.

Kavin helped Wesley onto Nibbles. "Wait here with the others," he told the boy. He mounted his own mare, then began to ride back to the execution site in order to retrieve the body of the king. Suddenly he turned and galloped back to the others.

"A battalion of the prince's guards is coming up the far hill and headed in this direction," gasped the captain, out of breath.

"But what of the king's body, sir?" asked one of the lieutenants.

"There is no time. We must be off at once. Ride, men, *ride!*"

The journey back *to* Orza was just as horrible as the journey *from* it earlier, except that now the horses were completely exhausted after having almost no rest whatsoever, and the men were bitterly despairing, having lost their commander-in-chief. Earlier there had been such an intense fear, but now fear had given way to utter despondency and hopelessness. The unthinkable had actually happened.

*****

Just before dusk that evening, the evil lord commanded several soldiers to return to the execution site with him in order that Reagale's body should be taken to the dungeon to rot there. He thought it would be a wonderful, cruel joke to taunt the prisoners with. He took a sort of twisted pleasure in the thought of dashing their hopes and crushing their dreams, and most of all, putting an end to their ridiculous myths and fairytales of a deliverer coming to rescue them from his clutches. He also thought it would add nicely to their torture to have the stench of a decaying body in their midst for a couple of weeks.

After having placed Regale's body on a large blanket, they carried him down into the dungeon of the palace and into one of the largest, most crowded cells. "I have heard of your rumors of deliverance. Here is your great deliverer! Let him deliver you now!" he wheezed, taunting his captives. "Put him up there, men! I think he'll make a nice centerpiece!" The guards lifted the limp body and placed it roughly on the flat stone slab in the middle of the room.

The flames from several mounted torches were casting mysterious dancing shadows on the cold stone walls of the dungeon. In the light of their eerie glow, Gabriella walked over to the still body, wondering what could have been the crime of this man whose face seemed so peaceful and kind but whose wounds showed that he must have been punished horribly and without mercy. Darius and his soldiers now gone, she gently stroked his ashen cheek, unaware that her little boy had kissed that same cheek only moments before, just beyond the prison walls. Finding a basin of water and a couple of rags nearby, Gabriella gently washed out his wounds, even though he was already dead. She then delicately wrapped his body in her worn, paper-thin shawl as a burial garment. Something inside her wished that she had known this man. Something inside her felt she did.

CHAPTER VI
Love's Mysterious Power

I t took quite a while for the Orzanian army to get back to their homeland, for the horses were tired and needed many breaks. But finally, after what seemed like an endless journey, they reached the city gates.

Once at home within the castle walls, a devastated and frightened Wesley ran straight to his room and locked himself in. The young boy slumped down into a heap on the floor and allowed grief to have its full way with him. Brianna and several others tried to no avail to get Wesley to come out. He would come out for no one, and he refused to be comforted or consoled.

Several hours passed. He lifted his head to wipe his bloodshot, swollen eyes on his shirtsleeve, and that's when he noticed it. The beautiful red rose, one of the two precious gifts that the king had given him so many months before, drooped limp and lifeless in its vase. This was the lovely flower that the king had cut from his garden especially for Wesley the day the child first arrived in Orza. When the king had breathed upon it, the rose had begun to radiate a strange and mysterious glow that never faded. But the many petals that had once adorned it were now fallen in a heap on the table beneath the vase, and it yielded no light whatsoever. "*Nooooooo!*" cried out Wesley with alarm. He jumped up and ran across the room to where the remains of his precious flower lay. He made a futile and pitiful attempt to pick up the petals, one at a time, with his shaking hands and try to reattach them to the bare head of the flower's stem, but to no avail. Each one simply fell lifeless again onto the tabletop. A fresh wave of grief swept over him.

Then he remembered the ring, the signet ring which he still wore on his thumb. This was another gift from the king when they arrived in Orza. The king had told him that anytime he wanted to see him, all Wesley had to do was kiss the ring and he would come to him. Without fail, every time Wesley had done this during the past year it had worked. The king would be there in an instant, jumping out from behind a tree, coming around the corner from another room, etc. It became a game to Wesley to try to figure out where he would appear.

He brushed the tears from his eyes and kissed the ring as he had done so many times before. But, of course, the king didn't come this time. Wesley waited for a long while, and then kissed the ring again. Many minutes passed, yet he found that he was still alone, all alone in the world once more. Wesley wept bitterly. All hope was *truly* gone.

*****

Three days later back in the prison in Trenza's capitol city...

The morning began as any other morning for the prisoners. Those who had found the refuge of sleep were awakened by the guards in cruel fashion. For some, this took the form of a crack on the head with a large stick. For others it might be a kick to the ribs, a dousing with a bucket of cold water, or various other methods meant to increase torment, torture and fear.

Once roused, the captives were herded into a single file line, shackled together at the ankles and forced through the dark passageways of the prison out into the central courtyard for the morning roll call. Although even the days in which the sun shone in this place were dismal, this morning the sky seemed very strange indeed. Heavy black clouds were rolling in fast, making a miserable morning into a very foreboding one. The eerie sky seemed to carry particular gloom and dreariness on its wings.

44

Saxron, the head guard, began calling out the names of the inmates. His steely eyes searched up and down the ranks to be sure all were accounted for. Saxron was no force to be reckoned with. He towered over six and one-half feet tall and was nothing but ripples of muscle with a large, bald head at the top of his very broad shoulders. He was as solid as any of the castle walls, and none of the prisoners ever even dreamed of trying to take on this menacing giant, especially when he was affectionately toting his favorite weapon of torture — a very long black leather whip with several sharp pieces of metal tied at the very tip. Many a prisoner had felt its bitter sting rip into their flesh, and many a prisoner had died from one too many strikes.

Saxron's all too familiar voice began the same raspy barking they were so accustomed to morning after dreadful morning.

"Tertius of Nikelos?"

"Here," came the weak reply.

"Friedman of Khandoor?"

"Here."

"Cynelle of Lyconis?"

"Yes."

"Simeon of Galixeos?"

"Here."

"Gabriella of Trent..."

But Gabriella did not have a chance to respond. For suddenly, and quite without warning, the ground beneath the courtyard's occupants began shaking ferociously with a violent earthquake. The entire castle swayed back and forth with the shifting earth. Amid shrieks and screams of terror, one could hear horrific cracking noises that sounded as if the very palace itself were ready to completely break apart and crumble to the ground. What lasted minutes felt like hours. Prisoners and guards alike were tossed off balance and found themselves looking up, bewildered, from the dusty ground of the courtyard, when the quake was finally over.

Earthquakes were fairly uncommon in these parts, so everyone was quite shaken on the inside as well as on the outside. The guards slowly tried to get their bearings back and regroup. They quickly finished roll, then hurriedly prodded the prisoners back to their underground home. When they were returned to the dungeon's main chamber, they found an amazing site; something which, fortunately, the guards had failed to notice in all their excitement. The stone slab where the stranger's body had been lying was split in two and was laid bare, all except for Gabriella's straggly shawl, which had been folded very neatly and laid back down. Terror filled the prisoners as they realized that they would probably be blamed for the disappearance of the man's body.

Suddenly, a strange, bright light filled the room. Everyone hid their eyes for a few moments until they adjusted and the strange light dimmed a bit. As they, one by one, removed their hands from their faces, they were utterly amazed. There before them stood the man himself, quite alive altogether. And they saw that he had in his right hand what looked like a giant set of keys; actually, they looked just like the keys that they had seen the guards use to open and lock the prison doors!

Walking over to the broken block of stone, he picked up Gabriella's shawl, then took it over and placed it back around her shoulders. "Thank you, dear lady, for your kindness," he said

softly. "Don't be afraid," said the man as he turned to the rest of the prison crowd. "I am King Reagale, of the land of Orza. I have come to rescue all of you who will follow me out of this place. I am the deliverer whom you have hoped for and dreamed of and," he turned to Gabriella once more, "whom some of you have sung about in the night. Who will follow me to my kingdom?" he asked, looking deeply into her blue eyes as if he saw right through to her heart.

"I will, my lord," she said without hesitation and knelt down on one knee. He reached down and gently lifted her chin so she could look at him once more. "I was hoping you would, Gabriella, for your son is there, and something tells me he would *really* like to see you," he smiled. The frail woman gasped with joy and tried to speak but could voice no sound, being overcome with emotion. As her eyes filled with tears, she fell at the feet of her new king and began to kiss them in her gratitude.

CHAPTER VII
The Homecoming

The king, now very much alive, led the newly freed prisoners through the inner catacombs of the dungeon. The people were amazed to see that the locks on the remainder of the chamber cells broke open and fell to the floor as he merely passed by each one. The growing crowd followed as he led them through the east passageway. Those who were stronger helped those who were sick or injured.

One of the armed guards sat stationed at the other end of this passageway. He was sitting on a bench sharpening one of his weapons and watching over a block of cells. Suddenly, he noticed the flame in the lantern which was on the bench beside him dancing wildly as a rushing wind moved down the corridor toward him. He looked up in the direction that the wind was coming from and saw the great crowd of escaped prisoners coming toward him led by the king. Now, you have to know that he was scared to death of the retribution which he was sure that these prisoners would exact upon him, being that he had taken great delight in beating and torturing them over the years. He let out a frightened shriek, dropped his weapons to the stone floor and fled as fast as his feet could carry him through the winding passageways to find someplace where he could hide from this mob.

The rather cumbersome group proceeded the rest of the way up the corridor to the foot of the long stairway which ascended to the first floor just inside the main palace doors. As they rounded the corner to the base of the grey stone stairs, there, in all his hideousness, stood Darius. Shrieks of terror rang out through the prisoners. The king turned to his company.

"Don't be afraid," he said, with both love and fire blazing in his royal eyes. "You all continue up the stairs and on to the main door. I will meet you there in a moment. I have some unfinished business to wrap up here." He flashed them a reassuring smile. One by one, the ex-prisoners pressed as closely to the staircase wall as possible and began their ascent.

Then the king turned his full attention back to the evil prince, whose face had gone ashen white with fright (and rightly so). Darius looked around frantically for a way of escape, but there was none. The trapped dictator walked backwards slowly until he found himself pinned up against the hard stone interior wall. He *knew* that Reagale was dead, because he had checked the body himself. How was it that he now stood before him — and *quite* alive!? His beady black eyes, once filled with hate, torture and death, were now filled with sheer terror, and he stood trembling in the presence of one he knew was far greater than himself.

After he was done dealing with the prince of darkness, King Reagale joined up with the others at the palace's main entrance. Some of the prisoners were trying unsuccessfully to open the doors that barred their exit. As they were not scheduled to be opened for another hour, the doors remained bound together with heavy chains and a large lock. They couldn't even budge them. Even if the prisoners could get the lock off, it would take all of their manpower combined to move them. The huge black doors were made of thick, solid iron and were extremely heavy. Most of the prisoners were simply too weak.

As the king walked toward the great doors, the crowd parted to let him through. He reached out and gently touched them with his forefinger, and the heavy metal doors fell to the ground with a great thud, sending a large cloud of dust up into the air and shaking the floor upon which they stood from the impact. A tremendous victory cry emerged from the people as they followed their new king through the wide entryway and out onto the front grounds of the palace.

The grand procession continued to pick up new followers as they made their way through Empiressen's city streets. People of all ages joined in the celebration march, leaving their homes behind them, their hoes in the field, their vendors' carts in the middle of the street. The king led the great parade through the city's imposing gates and in the direction of his kingdom.

*****

Meanwhile, back in Orza, the people were all still mourning the death of their beloved king. All business and commerce had ceased. All activities in the kingdom had stopped. Scarcely a soul could be found in the abandoned streets. All were in their houses with shutters closed tightly, doors locked, and all flags had been lowered to half mast. Anyone walking through the streets of the barren city listening closely could have heard the faint sound of weeping wherever they walked in the land. It was a city devastated, hopeless and very much afraid.

It was several days later before the great crowd, led by their new king, passed through the border of Orza and entered through Phyladel's gates. The former captives began to dance down the main street of the town, singing songs of liberation, deliverance and freedom as they came. One by one the townspeople, curious as to what all the commotion was, began cautiously opening the shutters and doors of their homes and poking their heads out to see what all the excitement was about. As soon as they saw their king was alive again, they lifted up a shout the likes of which has never been heard before or since. They poured out into the streets in force and joined in the dancing with all their might, lifting up a song of joy to the heavens! The grand procession slowly made its way toward the castle.

Back in the east wing of the palace, Wesley lay on his tear-soaked mattress, eyes swollen and red, with dark circles encompassing them. He had been mourning inconsolably these last days. He would not eat anything and refused to see or speak to anyone. Not only was his heart utterly broken by the death of his sweet king, but he was sure his own life was in grave danger as well. The evil prince, now that King Reagale was out of the way, would surely come back to claim his life as well.

That morning, Wesley awoke a little earlier than usual. Not at all that he *wished* to rise at this time, but there was suddenly a very bright light shining directly into his eyes. He assumed that someone must have entered his room as he slept and opened the shutters, which he had been keeping tightly drawn, and that it was the unhindered rays of the sun that were filling his room. Greatly annoyed, he rubbed the sleep from his eyes and started out of bed to go close them again. But he quickly realized that the light was coming, not from the window, but from the other side of the room entirely. Wesley pulled on his warm green robe and matching slippers, then walked over to investigate where this strange but brilliant light was coming from.

Wesley was amazed to find that the source of the radiating light appeared to be none other than the red rose. The flower, now even more beautiful than ever, was completely alive again. No longer limp and lifeless, it was standing upright and tall once more, spilling its lovely perfume in abundance, all petals restored to their proper places. It seemed as if there were even more on it than before! But, what did this mean? What could this possibly...

Suddenly, the boy was jolted out of thought by the faint sound of a familiar voice coming from outside his window. The voice was muffled coming through the closed shutters and the heavy, drawn drapes, but it sounded so much like...no, it couldn't be.

There...there it was again,

"Wesley, my son!"

What kind of cruel joke is someone trying to play?! thought Wesley. *First the flower, and now...could someone really be that vicious, especially in my time of mourning, to do something like this? But wait; there it is again,*

"Wesley, my son!"

Wesley ran to his window, quickly drew back the drapes, unlocked and threw open the shutters. There, standing in the courtyard just below his window, was...

It couldn't be! He had seen him *die*, had held his lifeless head in his lap, and had wept over his still, badly beaten body. But yet here he was gazing up, laughter on his face, at the incredible surprise he was giving this youngster whom he held so dear to his heart.

"Good morning, sunshine!" called the king.

"My Lord — Father — is it really, really you?!" exclaimed the boy.

"Why don't you come on down here and see!" The king laughed, and held his arms out to catch him as he had so many times before. Wesley, without a moment's hesitation, leapt onto the bronze dormer. In a flash he reached the edge and was airborne, and seconds thereafter he found himself in the strong, familiar arms that were waiting anxiously to catch him.

They clung to each other so tightly they could scarcely breathe! And now the tears that flowed were tears, not of sorrow or guilt, but of unbridled joy. The boy looked up through watery eyes into the king's kind face.

"Are you a...a ghost?" he asked, suddenly a trifle scared after hearing himself utter the word.

"No, my child, it is really me, in the flesh. See the scars where the rope cut deeply into my neck."

"But I still don't understand how... I mean, well... I *saw* you die!" stammered Wesley.

"My son, it was also written by the ancients that whenever a completely innocent one voluntarily dies on the behalf of a completely guilty one there begins a cosmic reversal of the forces of the dark magic that not even Prince Darius can stop. This had to take place, not only to free you and save your life, but also to free all the others who were in slavery to him," he gestured with his hand to the great crowd which had followed him all the way from Trenza. The king looked down at the boy again. "I love you, son."

"But *how* can you *possibly* love me after what I've done? I'm a *thief!*" Wesley dropped his head in shame.

"I took your place on that gallows, Wesley, and the penalty for your crime has, therefore, been paid in full. Don't ever forget this, my son. Now it is just as if you never committed the wrong. And you are now not a thief, but a beloved son to me — a son whom I love with all my heart!"

Wesley looked up into the eyes of this amazing, mysterious, wonderful man whom it seemed he had grown to love more and more with every passing day since their first meeting — a man he fully expected he would never see again. The boy reached up and gently touched the scarred, disfigured neck where the rope of execution had embedded its lasting imprint.

"Does it hurt?" he asked with concern.

"No, not any more. It just looks like it would."

"These scars look beautiful to me," said Wesley, "because it was by them that you set me free." But with a sudden realization he pulled away abruptly. "But, what about Prince Darius; won't he come back for you, and for me?"

"You don't need to have any fear of the wicked prince ever again. I have taken care of him."

Wesley looked with wide-eyed astonishment at the monarch. "Did you... *kill him?*" he asked hesitantly.

"Let's just say I took the teeth out of the lion and mercilessly declawed him. One day he and his will be completely destroyed by my father and me for all the wickedness they have done. But for now, I just took the bite out of him until that day comes!" he let out a hearty laugh.

"Now, my dear, dear Wesley, I have *another* surprise for you." He smiled broadly at the lad, then turned and motioned for the crowd to part and make way. "Do you remember what you told me you wanted most in the world?" Wesley looked deeply into the eyes of the king with a questioning look. The king cast his eyes toward the shifting mass of people before him and Wesley followed his gaze. Suddenly he caught sight of her — the mother he never thought he would see again. She was as beautiful to him as a vision, and at first he thought that's exactly what she might be. But regardless of whether this was a hallucination, vision, or a trick of his eyes, the little boy jumped out of the king's arms, bounded toward her and threw his tiny, little arms around her without reservation. The child buried his face in his mother's familiar neck. He stayed there for the longest time, and could only say one thing, which he repeated over, and over, and over..."*Oh, Mother!*" Even with her thin, dirt-smeared face, mussed hair and hands bruised and cut from hard labor, Wesley thought she had never looked more beautiful than she did right now — almost glowing, really. But, then again, that was what usually happened when anyone spent any length of time with his king, he had observed.

What a glad reunion it was! Reagale, being so moved in his own heart, came over and embraced mother and son and they all cried together (including many of the onlookers, for that matter) as if their hearts would break. There was scarcely a dry eye in the whole bunch!

The king finally lifted his head, wiped his eyes and spoke to the crowd. "Ah, what a day for joyous tears this has been, eh? I dare say we could have created another great sea with them all!" and they all laughed a long, hearty, from-your-toes laugh.

That day was the most joyous one Wesley could ever remember.   The three spent the remainder of it recounting some of the things from the past, catching up on what had taken place since the separation of mother and child and glorying in the events of the past week — tragedy turned triumph!

That night as Wesley prepared for bed, his mother came to tuck him in as she had so many times in the past. "Sing me that beautiful song you used to sing to me, mother. I missed you so much and would often hear you sing it to me in my dreams."

"Ah, but there is no need any longer, my son. For the song has been fulfilled. Our deliverer *has* finally come."

"You were right, mother. He did come for us and bring us with him to the land of the sun. I thought that was only a lullaby song. But to think, it was true!"

"Yes, it was true. But, how about if I sing you a new song? How would that be?"

Wesley shook his head and looked up into her big blue eyes. How he had missed her gentle, soft smile. Her lilting voice, which he remembered so affectionately, grew wings with each of the words which seemed to fold themselves round about him so comfortingly. She sang:

Little one, close your eyes
For this is the dawn of a better tomorrow
From the land of the sun our deliverer has come
And he rescued us all from our pain and our sorrow
Yes, with great joy he replaced all our sorrow

The needy he raised up from the ashes
And seated them high with kings and princes
Those who were dead he has given new life
Those who were blind have been given new sight
Yes, we who were blind now can see

And from now, my son, to the end of the age
We will bow down our knees to honor the one
Who has now come forth, upon his white horse
To take us with him to the land of the sun
To the City of Life with him, land of the sun

So may your sleep and your dreams be sweet
Let your little heart fill with hope evermore
For the promise fulfilled, our savior did come
Our new gracious king, our new glorious lord
Now sleep, sleep, sleep
Darling sleep, sleep, sleep
Sleep......sleep......sleep......

The three spent the rest of that wonderful week together walking and talking and laughing and reminiscing, and getting to know one another more deeply. Wesley often found himself during those first few days just staring at his mother, almost as if he was drinking in her image to make up for the time he had lost with her.

Several months passed. One day Reagale, Gabriella and Wesley were sitting in the garden gazebo. They were all trying to catch their breath after a little competitive run through the garden mazes.

"You two are too fast for me," laughed the king, winded. Truth be known, he really did always *let* them win.

"Wesley, you are getting better at it. I would say that next time *you* will be in first place," encouraged his mother. They paused for a few moments and took in the peaceful silence of their surroundings.

"Reagale, I've noticed that your wounds are still not healing very well," said Gabriella. "Perhaps I should get some balm to try to soothe and close them. They still do look so very sore."

"Thank you for your tenderness and caring heart toward me, but they will *never* heal, nor fade away — not with all the balm or medicine in the world. You see, dear one, they are not meant to. They are to remain in order to freshly bring to the minds of all whom I delivered on that day the full extent of what I did on their behalf. To some, these wounds will be an unsightly and horrid offense. Yet to others, they will signify the sweetness of life itself."

At this Gabriella fell silent. Amazed even more by this man that sat before her, she pondered yet again the great lengths he had gone to in order to save not only her little boy, but herself as well. She gave way to her overwhelming emotions and could simply contain her deep appreciation no longer. She began to sing a song which was birthed in the very core of her heart and welled up deep within her:

These scars which never fade
Remind me of the price you paid
To set us free when we were slaves;
And when my eyes behold these scars
These painfully deep and twisted scars
I see beauty in their every part
I see beauty...
I see love.

She kissed her hand and then placed it gently upon his disfigured neck. A tear fell from her eyes, spilling out of the ocean of gratitude which fully flooded her heart. "Thank you," she whispered.

It was a gloriously wonderful time, and Wesley could never remember being so happy. He had a wonderful new father and he also had his mother back. He was surrounded by those he loved most in the world and those who loved him most. He hoped that things would stay this way forever, not knowing that they were about to change yet again.

CHAPTER VIII
The Painful Parting

"Going away?" came Gabriella's broken voice, her eyes very anxious and full of questions.

"Please, my love, don't let your heart be troubled. And don't be afraid," said Reagale softly, stroking her cheek tenderly with the back of his hand, "for although it is necessary that I go, I will come back to bring you, Wesley and all the others with me when all is ready and right."

The small party of three had gathered in the palace library upon the king's request. Both Wesley and Gabriella were too shocked at the king's announcement to even reply. Everything had been going so wonderfully, like a dream that never ends. But now it *was* ending. Why would the king leave now, of all times?

Reagale looked at the two compassionately. "My dear ones, it is *good* for you both that I go. And I will return for you in just a short while—I give you my word." The air in the large room seemed to have turned stale and very heavy, like their hearts. Wesley thought it felt very much like someone was sitting directly upon his chest.

"*But why?* Why must you go and *leave us now?*" A tear trickled from Gabriella's eye, despite the fact that she was trying desperately to suppress it and show herself strong, especially for her son's sake.

Reagale brushed it away gently, then slipped a comforting arm around this woman whom he had come to love so deeply.

After a moment, he knelt to Wesley's level and asked, "My son, do you remember our great adventure on the Cliffs of Splendohr?"

"Yes, I will *never* forget," replied the boy, choking back the emotion that was forming a huge lump in his throat.

"Remember when I told you that I must return to Altierra one day, that I must go ahead of you to assist my father with the construction of the great city and to prepare a place for you...and for your mom?" He cast a tender glance up at Gabriella. "Do you remember, Wesley?"

"Yes, I remember."

"And do you remember what that place was like?"

"*Oh yes*, Father! I remember that there were walking paths that were made of shiny bricks of gold. And I remember that it was so beautiful there that I never wanted to leave, but we *had* to come back. There were huge fields and meadows filled with every kind of beautiful flower. And they smelled so much sweeter, and the colors were so much richer there. You would have loved it, Mother! And there were lots and lots of castles, I mean 'mansions,' all over the place. And you promised to build me one, too—right beside the skipping brook and the little grove of climbing trees!"

"So I did," laughed the king. "So I did!" He hoisted the lad up into his arms. "I *will* return to get you, and then I promise that we shall **never** again be apart." He looked deeply into Gabriella's tearful eyes. "I *promise* you. And when I take you back with me," he reached down and took her hand in his, "I would be honored if you would be my bride."

The flustered young woman's cheeks flushed with emotion, and for a moment she again found herself speechless. After several seconds she found her voice and replied, "Oh, yes, my dear. Yes.

For your love has captured my heart and I am yours alone. But, who am I that you should bestow such an honor upon me, a peasant girl, to be the wife of a king?"

"You, my dearest love, may still see yourself as a peasant girl; but when I look upon you, I see a queen already." He brushed another tear from her cheek, but this time it was a tear of joy.

"My love, you have sweetened my cup of sorrows this day. You have replaced the bitter anguish my soul felt at your leaving with the sweet, hopeful anticipation of your return. I shall *eagerly* await the day."

Wesley, still in the king's arms, let out a loud yelp of delighted approval! The king and his bride-to-be chuckled at the child's response to this exciting news, and the trio shared a warm embrace.

"And Wesley, once your mother and I wed, I plan to make you, publicly and officially, once and for all, my son!" Reagale grinned at Wesley, who was beaming from ear to ear, eyes shining with anticipation and delight. After giving him a squeeze, he set the lad down on the lush carpeted floor, then addressed mother and son once more.

"Until the day of my return, think of me often and remember my great love for you both. Also remember Altierra. Let its memory, as you recall it, carry and sustain you while I am gone and give you hope for the future...your future together with me forever. But now, come, for I must announce my departure to the others and give instructions for the furtherance and care of the kingdom in my absence." The king gingerly took them each by the hand, and they walked together slowly toward the throne room.

The great hall was filled once more; wall-to wall with people, each one wondering what the news could be that was about to be announced, wondering why they had been summoned here today. The king's messengers had simply conveyed that they were to gather in the throne room at eight o'clock that evening for an extremely important address by the king. Perhaps the monarch was embarking upon another rescue mission for a couple of weeks. Perhaps he intended to honor one of their contemporaries for noble service to His Lordship.

As the trio entered, a still hush fell upon the room and, one by one, everyone bowed in respect for their great leader. Gabriella and Wesley were seated off to the side as the king took his seat upon the throne, from which he began his address to the crowd.

"My dear people, my news today is bittersweet. Bitter because I must leave you for a little while." A low murmur could be heard throughout the great hall as people speculated to each other as to where the king could be going this time.

"I have been called to return to my father to assist him in the building of the great city, Altierra," the people once again fell silent, "and to prepare a place for each and every one of you there. It is bitter because, although I will be sending Troan to assist you and to bring messages back and forth between us, I long in my heart even before my parting for the day when we will all again be face to face. It is sweet, however, because I go to make ready a place for you, that where I am you may come and dwell with me forevermore. And know in your hearts that I will indeed return to bring you back with me in just a short while. It is sweet because on that day we will never again be apart; sweet because, as wonderful as Orza is, the glorious splendor of Altierra is like nothing you have ever dreamt or imagined, and I am filled with great joy in anticipation of taking you there with me. So, do not mourn — but rather, hope. Hope in the day to come; wait for it, look for it, long for it.

Until that day, I am appointing my most trusted and loyal men to assist in protecting and ruling this great kingdom on my behalf until I return. Will the following men please rise and come forward for commissioning: Connor Fitzpatrick, Limpett Dearling, Norpid Dearling, Truffle Dearling, Kavin Klauss, Christias Niles, Trey Farquas, Tameric Bastian, Doctor Peter Emerson, Abdi Meraz, Finley O'Malley and my dear son, Wesley." Wesley was startled when he heard his own name being announced. Surely he was too young to be of any importance and value to the kingdom.

"Go forward, son," coaxed his mother proudly. "Your father is calling you for service!"

One by one they filed up and knelt before the king. Once they were all assembled in front of the throne, he drew his sword from its sheath and placed it on each man's shoulder in turn, saying, "A knight I dub thee this day. May love, honor and loyalty be your guiding principles. Be true to the king and be true to his ways evermore, and act with wisdom and kindness in his name."

When Reagale came to Wesley, he placed the heavy metal sword down a little more gently, then made the same pronouncement with a loud voice so that all in the great room could hear unmistakably. He bent over and followed the ritual with a tender kiss to the cheek, then whispered in the young child's ear, "My dear, dear Wesley, don't let *anyone* look down on you because you are young. I love you, son, and I am so proud of you." The lad's face beamed until it threatened to break into pieces if he grinned any harder.

"Although I am leaving, I will not leave you alone, my good people," the dignitary stood and addressed the greater crowd once more. "After a couple of days I will also send to you my most trusted friend and faithful messenger, Troan. Honor him as you honor me, for he will be sent to you in my name and will bear my authority. I want you to stay in the castle for the next few days and wait for his arrival. It won't be long. He will comfort and help you and will also bring you messages from myself and my father. You can, in return, give him messages to bring back to us. I will keep in close contact with you through him. Don't be downhearted or afraid. Remember that it is for your good that I go, and I shall return in due time! Though the day seem to tarry, keep careful watch, and wait for me. I promise you with all of my heart, my beloved ones, that I will return for you.

Until then, be steadfast, immovable, always abounding in the work of your king, knowing that your toil is not in vain that you do in my name. Be ever on the alert, stand firm, act like men and be strong. Now is the time for bravery; now is the time for fearless courage. Fight hard to continue my work here, and persevere in pushing back the borders of Trenza. Rescue as many as are willing from the evil clutches of Darius.

I am also leaving Kavin, Captain of the Guard, and all of his troops here to watch over you all. There will be battles to fight, territory to take, and there will be more captives to free. My Wesley, who once was one of these captives, is so very precious to me." He hoisted the boy up. "But there are more Wesleys to be rescued, begging along the roadsides of Trenza for a half-pence or a crust of bread. Go to them in the name of the King of Orza and bring them out! I love you all!"

A great cheer arose from the crowd. The ruler waved farewell to his loyal subjects, then turned and dismissed himself, Gabriella and Wesley close by his side. He had asked Connor to go ahead of them, saddle his horse and meet them at the southern gate.

They continued down the hallway toward the appointed meeting place. The reality of Reagale's very imminent departure began to dawn upon the lad. Although the youngster tried to suppress his emotions, as his heart grew heavier and heavier he found himself giving way to the surge. The king couldn't help but hear the sniffling and quiet sobs. He stopped and stooped down to brush a giant tear from Wesley's cheek with his hand. "Please don't cry, dear," said the ruler softly. He brought Wesley near and held him in a tight embrace. Wesley buried his head in the king's chest.

After a few silent moments, he stood up, still holding the somber lad. He took Gabriella's hand and drew her closer. He could see the pain and sorrow that marked her face, too. "My heart breaks as well, my dear ones, for I will miss you more deeply than you could ever possibly imagine. You will be on my heart and in my thoughts day and night. But I *must* go, and now is the time. Wesley, you are a big nine-year-old boy now. And this, above all, is a time for courage and bravery."

"Yes, Father." Wesley sniffed a couple of times and wiped his eyes.

"And son," he looked earnestly into the boy's eyes, "I have already informed Connor of my desire that *you*, being my son and heir, be the one to see to all of my affairs and look after the running of the kingdom until I return. Wesley, I'm leaving you in charge."

Wesley's eyes grew wide as saucers. "Me?! You want to leave *me* in charge? But, I'm only a little boy, Father! What I mean to say is...well, I don't know how to run a country. I would sure mess things up real good!—I mean real *bad*! One of the others, like Connor or Kavin, would do so much better!" he exclaimed incredulously.

"But it is *you* that I want, my son. Through Troan I will communicate with you often, and I will teach you all you need to know. I will train your hands for war, for war there will be. But don't be afraid, for I will give you all the instruction you need. And, although you will not see me, dear one, I will answer you every time you call to me. I am also leaving you all the wise counselors, advisors and helpers you could ever want for." With this he loudly clapped his hands two times, and the scuffle of several feet could be heard approaching. Beside them a large oak door that led to one of the castle's many lower chambers opened, and out poured Trey and Brianna, Kavin, Tameric, Doctor Emerson, Christias, Abdi and Finley, as well as the three beloved dwarfs, into the red carpeted hallway.

Christias edged his way to the front. "I speak on behalf of all present when I say from the bottom of my heart that we are completely at your service, young Wesley, and will help you in any way that we possibly can. We will serve you faithfully and loyally, just as we served our lord, your father."

"Here, here!" chimed in the others. The motley crew bowed to show their allegiance to the lad.

The overwhelmed Wesley, face flushed with excitement and fear, extreme joy and bitter sorrow, simply said, "Thank you...."

The convoy escorted the monarch through the corridor and out a side door at the castle's southern end. "The time has come now for me to go. Connor is waiting for me with Silver at the south gate. I will ride to the Cliffs of Splendohr, and then Troan will escort me home to Altierra from there. Then, just as I said, I will send Troan to you as a helper. He will teach you all things and bring to your remembrance all that I have spoken to you and taught you. I will send him to you in three days. Wait for him. He will give you further instructions from me."

"Pardon me, My Lord, but how will we recognize Troan when he comes? After all, none of us have ever met him," piped in Limpett.

"Trust me, dear friend, he is *very* unusual, and you will know him when you see him," the king gave a little chuckle, anticipating their reaction when they met the strange, yet glorious, winged creature for the first time. He turned once more to Gabriella and Wesley. "I love you both with all my heart." His words pierced their hearts to the very core. "Do not despair. Remember, I will come for you soon, and we will be face to face once more. Then nothing — *nothing* will ever part us again!" He kissed them both and held them tightly one final time. Then they watched him walk down the pathway away from the castle, his red silk traveling cloak rippling like shimmering waves behind him. They watched his figure become shadowy as he walked further from the light of the castle, then dark, then it disappeared completely, swallowed up in the blackness of the night. Wesley thought it suddenly seemed much darker and that it suddenly felt much colder, and he shivered with the chill of it. His mother knelt down and placed her shawl around his shoulders. Together they wept there in the night.

CHAPTER IX
The Mysterious Visitor

aylight dawned the third day. Wesley rubbed the sleep from his eyes, tossed back the blue cotton throw which covered him, and sat up on the rectangular mat upon which he had been sleeping for the past couple of nights. He looked around the throne room for other signs of life. He was surprised to see that mostly everyone, including his mother, had already wakened. Only a couple of other children still lay sleeping. All of the king's closest friends and most loyal subjects had been gathered together in this room since he took his leave. They were, according to his instructions, waiting upon the arrival of the messenger which had been promised. Though none knew quite what to expect, there was an air of excitement about the place, like electricity that filled the great room and seemed to charge everything and everyone with spine-tingling enthusiasm and anticipation. They all still missed the king's presence sorely, to be sure. But, at the same time, they were anxiously awaiting the fulfillment of his great promise to them.

Wesley stood and rolled his mat, then put it in a pile in one corner of the great room with several others. He went over to where Gabriella was standing and talking with Brianna and two of the other ladies.

"Well, good morning, my little sleepyhead!" Gabriella said playfully, kissing her son on the forehead.

"Good morning, Mom," replied the still semi-bleary-eyed youngster. "When did you wake up?" he asked in the midst of a combination big-mouthed yawn and refreshing stretch.

"Well, actually, we stayed awake all night after we put you kids to bed," she said with a sheepish, childlike grin. "We were all much too excited to sleep."

"Hey, that's not fair! Can I stay up all night sometime?" Wesley yawned again.

His mother laughed and teasingly ruffled his hair. "It seems to me, son, that you can barely function on a full night of sleep! How could you expect to handle the king's affairs if you had none at all?! Now, why don't you go wash up and fix your hair. When the messenger comes today you certainly don't want him to catch you looking like you just crawled out from under a rock!" The grinning boy set off for the washroom posthaste, and the ladies resumed their conversation. They were recounting all of the wonderful memories they had had with the king, all the wonderful things he had said and done.

Wesley returned a couple minutes later, looking quite a bit more well-kempt than he had previously. "Mother, do you really think he will come today?" he asked excitedly.

"Well, my love, our beloved ruler did say three days. And I have never known him to break his promises; have you?"

"No, never." Wesley's eyes grew big, and his heart beat faster in his chest. What would this mysterious visitor be like?

Breakfast on this particular morning remained largely uneaten by those gathered in the throne room. They had been eating all of their meals together since "The Parting," as they now referred to it. Everyone seemed too excited to think about their stomachs — everyone except for Wesley, that is. Oh, he was just as excited as everybody else, but he wasn't about to let it spoil his appetite. He was just about to bite into his third cheese bun when he heard a familiar sound, one that had replayed in his dreams many a night.

It was distant at first, then steadily growing louder and louder, the sound of a rumbling earthquake, or of a ravaging tornado. He remembered this sound from his experience at the cliffs with the king. No wind this time, just deafening sound. Suddenly, the room filled with a blinding light! Some fell to the ground before its brilliance. Others covered their eyes and turned away.

After a couple of moments, the noise began to lessen and the light began to dim a bit in its intensity. Wesley slowly removed his hands from over his eyes and looked up toward the throne to see what the source of the light was. It was still pretty bright, but he could faintly make out the shape of some type of large beast. It definitely wasn't the shape of a man, but more of an animal of some kind, or so it appeared from what little he could see.

As the light continued to fade, Wesley could see that it appeared to be an incredible being, with the body of a very large white horse, yet with the head of a man. As Wesley looked on, he saw the creature unfold and spread out what appeared to be massive wings on either side of his body. The span of his wings was no less than twenty feet from tip to tip.

The hush that had fallen over the room at the start of this manifestation still remained, and those gathered looked on in stunned silence. Although they had all *heard* of Troan, none of them had ever actually *seen* Troan. He was quite a bit different in appearance than what they had expected or imagined!

"Faithful ones who love the king, do not be afraid," his deep, penetrating voice echoed through the chambers of the castle, as well as the very chambers of their hearts. "I am here to help you and to comfort you, to assist you, to bring courage to your hearts and strength to your hands for the battle that lies before you." With every word Wesley felt as if he himself was somehow growing taller and stronger on the inside. He felt less and less like a little nine-year-old boy, and more and more like a bold young man preparing to wage war upon the enemy.

"I will bring you messages from the king, and will take yours to him, as well. I will instruct you and aid you in completing the assignments that the king has designated for each one of you. I will also gift you with powers such as he himself displayed while he walked among you. I will teach you all things and help you to remember all the words which the king spoke to you. I will stay with you always, to guide and help you until the king himself comes back to take you all to your final destination—the land of Altierra."

Mouths hung open in stark wonder and reverent awe of the magnificent winged creature. One by one, the king's subjects bowed before their glorious visitor.

In the days and months ahead, they would get to know and love this mysterious being. He would guide them with great insight and wisdom and would also make known to them the will of the king when they were unclear on how to proceed in a matter. The king would also send his messenger with notes to his precious bride-to-be, expressing his undying love and his anxiousness to be with her again. Gabriella longed for that day. And, of course, there was always a special note just for Wesley, to encourage him in the wonderful job he was doing managing the king's affairs and just to let him know he missed the lad greatly. Wesley looked forward to these letters beyond measure. It was the next best thing to actually being with the king, and it would have to due for now.

CHAPTER X
Battle Cry!

"We have gathered here this afternoon in order to solidify our battle plans, and to prepare for first strike." The meeting room echoed with Troan's powerful, unmistakable voice. Wesley, Connor, Limpett, Norpid, Truffle, Trey, Christias, Tameric, Abdi, Doctor Emerson, Finley and Kavin were all present and accounted for. The table around which they all sat seemed to symbolically represent this mishmash, hodgepodge bunch—polished seemingly to perfection, yet those who ventured close enough could see that it was still a bit rough around the edges.

"Firstly, Kavin—please update the others on what you informed me of earlier regarding how the enemy is mobilizing."

"Yes, Sir. I just received a report this morning from one of our troops who risked his very life to get us this information. It seems that Darius's army makes ready to attack as we speak. They have moved great numbers of men down into the Ravine of Amar on the northeast side of Lyconis. They have also moved another sizeable company into a large wooded glen on the southeastern tip of Nikelos, beside Southside Bay. According to my informant, it appears that they are planning a surprise attack on Phyladel, Ephesac and Pergamun. The people of Trenza have been indoctrinated by Darius that the king's followers stole his body from the dungeon and brought him back here to be buried. Darius and only a handful of his officials (who have been sworn to secrecy upon penalty of death) know the truth about what happened. Now, word has reached Darius somehow that Reagale is really gone, that he has left Orza, and he thinks that the country has been

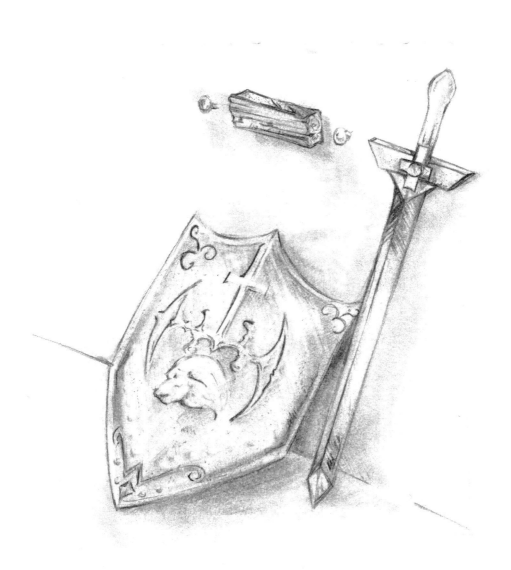

weakened by the king's absence and has become vulnerable prey. It seems that they plan to make haste with their attack on these three main cities and that they then anticipate the swift surrender of the other provinces. My source overheard some of the soldiers talking about orders that had been issued by Darius to slaughter every man, woman and child in these three cities in order to prevent any resistance from the remaining ones."

The whole room fell into a horror-induced hush which lasted several moments. Utter outrage burned in each man's eyes.

"That *BEAST*!!!!" Connor was the one to finally break the silence.

"What should we do, Troan?!" asked a panicked Wesley, as his mind flashed to his dear mother.

"Yes! It is obvious that we must move *posthaste*, Troan. Tell us, Counselor, what would you have us do?!" added Christias.

"Steady, men. Do not let yourselves be anxious or afraid. Rather, be strong and brave, men of action, courage and valor. Remember who you serve, remember why you serve and remember who will lead you to victory. The one whom you fight for and who's emblem you bear on your shields and who's name you each bear on your hearts is greater—far, far greater!

Now, as far as *our* strategy: it is critical that we launch a swift preemptive attack. We do have an advantage in that they still believe that we are completely unaware of their plans.

Christias, I am placing you in charge over divisions one through fifty. You will need to organize your men immediately and head north, to the wooded hills just before the Valley of Kidron on the far side of Ephesac. But you must make haste, for the enemy advances as we speak, and it will take you some time to travel that distance. You will need to reach the hills and get your divisions set for battle before Darius's troops reach the edge of the Mountains of Tyre. We anticipate their arrival there sometime tomorrow afternoon. When Darius's troops reach the end of the range and begin their descent into the valley, you will be able to fell many with the quiver before they even start up the other side. While in the barren valley, the enemy will be entirely exposed and vulnerable. The thick cover of the trees in which you will be embedded should help hide your presence and position in the hills until it is too late and they are trapped in the valley. However, if you have not arrived and positioned yourself for an offensive before they pass through the valley, it will be much more difficult to prevent them from penetrating the inland.

Kavin, you will lead the remaining forty-eight divisions through the Fields of Jaar and down to South Beach along the Silver Sea. You will position yourselves near the Cliffs of Splendohr. You will probably do well to have some of your men holding the beachhead at sea level, but plan to have the greatest number up on the cliffs to implement the same strategy which I commissioned Christias to use. You will have the cover of cliff and tree from there and definitely the advantage. You will need to see to it that the enemy does not make it through the Fields of Jaar and into the city. Although you do not have as far to go, please do not delay in organizing and preparing. Remember, the enemy thinks that we are unaware of his tactics and advances. We want to be ready and to have the element of surprise against him.

Meanwhile, I will get a message to the king to make him aware of our plight and petition for help. Again I say, don't be afraid. Be men of courage, men of valor! And remember, help always comes when you need it the most and expect it the least.

Now, I send you forth in the good name of our king. Go...and God speed!"

No one delayed in following Troan's instructions. As the faces of their wives, children and other loved ones flashed before their eyes, each man realized only too well how much was at stake here. Faces were stern; actions were swift and purposeful. War was upon them, and danger was near.

It took only ninety minutes for Christias to make ready his divisions. Kavin was actually ready to move his men out a couple of minutes before them. He seemed to always have a plan and a strategy to implement in any given situation. He was as skilled a leader and commander as ever there was.

As the troops marched out in separate directions to prepare to meet their enemy in battle, a keen observer could see the same thing in each of their eyes — a look of fierce devotion and desperate, protective love that was birthed in the core of each heart. Nothing can stand against such an army who fights from the depths of their hearts, because they fight on a whole different level, a completely different plane. They fight not out of hate — they fight for love. But would it really be enough?

CHAPTER XI
The Vanishing

I t had been a weary day of battle, indeed. Three weeks had passed since the onset of war. And, although the Orzanian troops had so far been able to prevent the enemy from entering the city, they weren't sure how much longer they could hold them back.

Sweat and blood mixed on all too many of the soldiers' drenched, torn clothing. If they were lucky, the blood was not their own, but that of an enemy soldier slain at their hand. The merciless heat of the sun had not helped, beating down unrelentingly upon the battle-weary fighters. Never had the combat seemed bleaker, and never had the battle seemed more hopeless than it had on that day.

When Company Fifty-Seven finally found themselves back at the camp, most of the men fell onto the flimsy mats within their tents in sheer exhaustion, Wesley among them. Although quite too young for combat, it had been altogether impossible for Wesley's advisors to keep him away from fighting on behalf of his father, the king, and also fighting to protect his mother whom he loved so desperately. Small of stature and weak with regards to physical strength as he was, he had proven himself to be extremely tenacious and brave thus far in battle. It seemed that whenever he went out to engage the enemy some unseen force was watching over him and fighting for him. He had some amazing and unexplainable victories for a "knight" of his age. Kavin also made sure the other soldiers watched out for "the young one," as he affectionately called him.

Today, however, had been an extremely difficult day for young Wesley. At one point, when the afternoon had been its hottest, he had become very dizzy and faint and had to be carried off the field until he regained his composure and strength. Now that night had come, he was very glad to be back inside his khaki-colored tent with his lumpy, makeshift bed, and he found himself asleep before he even realized he had lain down.

By about ten o'clock that night, the camp was beginning to look like a ghost town. Although a scattered one could be found cleaning his weapons or eating his meager dinner by the fire, many of the men had simply collapsed with exhaustion in their tents. Wesley had turned in at about a quarter to ten. He had been asleep for a couple of hours when he was awakened with a start by a strange noise. The war had made all of the men—and boys—just a bit jumpy, you see. One never knew when the enemy might become bold enough to attempt a night raid. And Wesley was very much aware that his tent was on the very outskirts of the camp and closer than he would rather be, when sound asleep, to the enemy's position. He'd had more than one nightmare about a night raid and being dragged out of bed and either captured or killed. These were the kind of nightmares that make your heart race furiously in your chest, make you gasp or cry out in your sleep and cause you to break out in a cold sweat that drenches your clothes and bedding. Wesley thought that maybe he was still asleep and again at the mercy of his own fearful imagination.

There was a fairly loud scratching sound right beside his head on the westward side of the tent. Something was scratching with purpose against the canvas. "Whhh...who...who's there?!" Wesley tried, without success, to sound brave and authoritative, but ended up just sounding like a scared little boy. The scratching ceased, but now he heard footsteps...no, it sounded more like the hooves of an animal. Wesley sat up and peered through the dark, trying to follow the sound's movement with his eyes. He pulled his thin blanket (which was making a feeble attempt at keeping him

80

warm, let alone protecting him from the danger outside) tighter up under his chin. The sound rounded the corner to the front of Wesley's tent, then stopped just in front of the opening. Wesley, now frightened beyond measure and unable to see anything at all in the blackness, quickly reached down and groped for the sword that lay beside him on the dirt floor. He found his weapon and held it up in striking position. Eyes big and full of fear, he fought desperately to try to see his possible foe through the impenetrable blackness of night. His quivering left hand still clutched the blanket up around his neck as the young boy waited for his would-be enemy's next move.

"Wesley," called a familiar and very welcomed voice in a loud whisper. Wesley strained to hear. The voice called out again, "Wesley!" Wesley ran toward the tent's opening, stumbling over a few mislaid items on the way, and threw back the flap.

"Troan...Troan...is that you?"

"In the flesh, my valiant young warrior!" chided the king's aid.

"Am I ever glad to see you! You *scared* me out of my *wits*!" exclaimed Wesley, dropping the sword to the ground and throwing his arms around his wonderful, beastly friend. Troan nuzzled the boy's neck, returning the warm greeting.

"Take the torch out of my saddlebag and light it." Wesley did as his friend instructed and held the torch up to get a better look at Troan's sweet, familiar face. "I know you are glad to see me, little one, but I brought a friend with me whom I think you may be even more delighted to set your tired little eyes upon..."

Surely he would not have brought my mother to the battlefield! Reasoned the lad to himself.

And then, from around the corner of the tent, stepped the king.

"*Ohhhh!*" cried out Wesley, and, dropping the torch to the sandy ground, he ran and jumped up into the ruler's arms. The two hugged for a long while, just enjoying being together again. An embrace is never so sweet as when one has gone without it for a long time.

"Wesley, my son, the time has come, the appointed time that you've been waiting for," said the dignitary in a hushed tone. Wesley looked up into his eyes, trying to grasp exactly what he was saying. "The construction of Altierra is finally complete. I can't wait for you to see it," said Reagale with a twinkle in his eye. "It's time to go from this place, for you, as well as for all my other loyal subjects and those who have chosen the side of the emperor and me."

Wesley could hardly believe his ears. Could it be true?

"You will ride with me on Troan, and all the others will follow close behind. And now, let us go, my son." And with that, the monarch tightened his grip around the child's waist and swung up into the saddle which had been fastened securely around Troan's midsection.

A great wind had begun to stir in the camp, the kind of wind that comes before a spectacular storm. The turbulence had begun kicking up great clouds of sand into the air. This wind had a familiar feel to Wesley, and he wondered if...

Whuuusssshhhh, off they bounded into the night sky. Wesley was amazed at the strength Troan had to be able to carry both him and the king with what seemed to be so little effort. He held tightly to Reagale as they increased in altitude, but at the same time peered over his shoulder to watch the world he had known so

well grow smaller and smaller beneath him. The threesome soon leveled out from their steady climb and headed farther out to sea.

Wesley enjoyed feeling the wind running its cool fingers through his dusty brown hair, causing it to flap wildly in every direction. His mind raced with exciting thoughts of the adventures and joys that awaited him once they reached their destination. He thought about the fact that he would finally be able to meet the emperor face-to-face. What would he be like? What should a little boy say when he first meets a great sovereign for the very first time? Hmmmm... *Your Highness,* Wesley rehearsed in his mind while imagining himself bowing gracefully. *It is a pleasure to make your Lordship's acquaintance, O Great Emperor...* maybe a bit wordy and overdone. *Your Magnificence... Your Majesty...Your Grace...Your Eminence...* Wesley pondered all of the possible scenarios for the entire remainder of their journey.

*****

Meanwhile back in Phyladel, Gabriella was busy in the castle with Brianna, shredding old clothing in order to make bandages for those who had been wounded in battle. Because the castle was so large a building and was so strategically located, being the closest structure of significant size to the front lines of the battle at South Beach, it had become a perfect place for a hospital for the injured. Many had sought and found refuge and help there in the tender and compassionate hands of these two ladies. They were warriors in their own right, to be sure.

It was getting late now. It had been a very long, weary day, and they were still not close to being able to turn in. Another cart with wounded soldiers had just pulled in from the front about one hour before, and there were still at least five men in need of emergency assistance that hadn't yet been treated.

83

Brianna was applying a salve bandage to a wounded leg. She wiped the blood which covered her once lovely, delicate hands on her white nurse's apron, adding more red to the very colorful, smeared design which covered the front of it. Then she used her sleeve to wipe the sweat from her forehead, trying to push back some of the strands of hair that had fallen from under her cap during the grueling duties of the day.

"More boiling water needed over here right away, Connor!" cried Brianna. "And more gauze!"

"It's on the way!" came the reply.

Gabriella hurried over to the other side of the room to examine the injured that had just been brought in. "Limpett! Oh dear, it's Limpett! Someone help me!" A few workers rushed over and carefully lifted poor Limpett onto a stretcher, then from the stretcher onto a cot. "He's unconscious and seems to be bleeding internally," said Gabriella anxiously to the young man that was assisting her. She leaned over to examine her newest patient and dear friend. "Limpett...dear, dear Limpett..." she whispered. The limp figure had some fresh blood trickling from his right ear and from his mouth. The prognosis did not look good.

"We must figure out where he is bleeding from and try to find a way to stop it immediately," she said, her voice quaking but firm with resolve. "I propose we begin by..."

Just then there was a loud and violent rumbling, and the castle began to shake. There was the sound of falling jars crashing against the hard stone floor and breaking into thousands of tiny clay and glass shards. There was the sound of metal surgical instruments and trays hitting the floor. Gasps of shock mingled with cries of fear went up throughout the makeshift treatment center. The violent trembling continued for what felt like several minutes. Gabriella grabbed onto the side of Limpett's cot in order to steady herself and keep from falling.

Just then, a great wind whipped from the corridor into the great hall, blowing around anything that wasn't battened down. "Someone close the front doors and all the windows, quickly!" cried Brianna.

"But they are already shut," said Connor, bewildered.

"What is happening?!" Brianna's voice quivered. "Something dreadful, I fear."

"No, something *wonderful*," whispered Gabriella. "Something wonderful..." And then they were gone.

CHAPTER XII
Deadly Silence

"Tonight will be the night," rasped out General Lanos, leader of the army of the dark side.

"Do you have a strategy?" asked one of the other ten high-ranking officials who were seated in the large mess tent in the center of Darius's camp, just west of South Beach.

"Of *course* I have a strategy!" Lanos barked at the surly and brutish man. "We shall divide our troops into thirds, sending one third to position themselves on each side of the enemy camp—west, north and east. Then we shall send out small companies of scouts to eliminate any enemy soldiers that are keeping watch. We will give them twenty minutes to complete their assignment. Then, upon my signal, we will rush upon our sleeping victims and slay them before they even know what hit them."

"And what is to be your signal, General?" asked Captain Helos.

"I shall give six short blows on the horn of a ram, followed by one long blow, and then we charge. Go and inform your men. Have them turn in early, as they are already at the point of exhaustion from the hardship of the day's fighting and we must wake them at one o'clock this morning to prepare for the night's— ummm, how shall I say— **festivities**," he hissed through an evil smile. "We will pull out of camp at about two o'clock. Each man will bring with him only his sword, bow and a quiver of arrows. We must remain stealthy, quick and light of foot for our surprise attack. This war will end *tonight*!"

The company dispersed, each leader going in a different direction to spread through the ranks word of the events that were to take place in a few short hours. Only Lanos and Darius remained behind.

"We move from the enemy's camp directly to their cities and begin the slaying of *all* Orzanians, military as well as civilians. I want every man, woman and child *dead*, Lanos. That is an order," spat Darius cruelly. "No captives whatsoever. I want total and complete destruction of the enemy." He leaned forward, close enough that Lanos could feel the hot, rancid breath against his face, Darius's steely eyes boring right through him. "Do I make myself clear, General?" he snarled slowly and purposefully.

"Yes, My Lord," said Lanos, in quite a more fearful tone than one would expect from a man of his rank and position. Lanos understood one thing *very* clearly. Darius had loyalty to no one. He would just as soon have his own mother sent to the gallows as Lanos. He was demanding, capricious, conniving and a very, very dangerous man. He rather enjoyed making examples of people. The general decided he would not like to be one of them. Do *exactly* as you are told and don't ask any questions, and you'll likely stay alive. This was the motto he had come to live by. He hoped it held true, for his sake.

The plan proceeded without variation. Darius's men were awakened in the middle of the night at one o'clock. The exhausted, bleary-eyed men began assembling their gear and weaponry. Most of them had slept in the same clothes they had fought in the day before in honor of the much abbreviated night's sleep. They trickled out of their tents and began to reorganize themselves into their ranks. The troops were quickly divided into three groups. One third was assigned to head to each of their respective positions on the north, west and east sides of the Orzanian camp.

By a quarter to two they were ready to head out. With Lanos fast in the lead, mounted on his white and black peppered mare, the rest of the army followed aggressively. The hillside was soon covered with a moving blanket of black and silver, the air filling with the thundering of hooves. Darius, riding on his own black stallion, had hung back from the others with a small group of soldiers. He figured he would give his army several hours to do their grueling task, and then he would come to survey their work and to see how they had fared in the battle. He also preferred to stay a bit behind in order to slay with his own sword any of the cowardly among his ranks who should become faint of heart and attempt to turn back.

When they were yet about one mile away from the enemy camp, Lanos sent the Special Forces companies on ahead. Then he split the troops and sent them in their appointed directions. The men tried to ride as silently as possible at this point, as the element of surprise was what they were relying upon for a sure and quick victory. Some of the men stole through the woods which bordered the camp on the west, while others continued beyond the woods and over the grassy, heather-covered slopes hemming it in to the north, and some stole down onto the sandy beach to the east. Lanos himself joined the battalion headed east of the camp. He counted approximately twenty minutes and then, once he was fairly certain that the enemy watchmen had been eliminated and the rest of his men were all in position, he reached down into the satchel of his saddle and pulled out his ram's horn. Raising the horn to his sun-cracked lips, he gave six short but forceful blows, followed by one long.

About ten seconds later it started...a faint rumble which seemed to come from every direction and grew moment by moment in intensity until the very ground beneath shook with the force of the rushing army. As the soldiers drew nearer to the Orzanian camp, each dismounted from his horse, drew his sword,

and began ripping open, one by one, the hundreds of tents that
were lined up closely together.

Lanos waited on the camp's edge, still mounted on his horse,
overseeing the battle. He peered into the deep darkness of the
night. The moon was but a slit in the sky and was not gracing them
with much of its light on this particular eve, therefore making it
very difficult to see. He listened intently to try to assess what was
happening. He waited for several minutes, hoping to hear the cries
and screams as the enemy awoke to the terror that awaited them.
But he heard none. He could hear only the footsteps of his soldiers
running to and fro, the sound of swords ripping open the many
canvas tents, a bit of banging about as his night-blinded men
tripped over pots, pans, and other metal objects and then...silence.

Lanos decided to enter the camp himself to see what was
going on. As he drew nearer he heard one after another of his men
whispering, "There's no one in here, either...or in any of these." In
fact, it soon became apparent that the entire camp of the enemy lay
empty — *completely deserted!* And it appeared that they had left in
somewhat of a hurry. Kettles had been left boiling over small fires
(which by this time of the night were merely glowing embers), and
in some of the tents they entered there were plates of half-eaten
food and personal valuables lying about, abandoned. It also
appeared that they left by foot, because all of their horses were still
tied to their hitching posts.

*What could all of this possibly mean? A whole entire army doesn't
just up and disappear! What kind of magic is at work here?* thought
Lanos trembling, trying to process it all.

A dark, sickening feeling began to grow in the pit of his
stomach. He wondered, with mounting fear, how Darius would
react to this news. The prince of Trenza was not due to arrive on
the scene for a while and was still completely unaware of the
perplexing situation in which his soldiers found themselves.

Darius was known for his fierce temper. When he discovered that the enemy had escaped, would he seek to exact revenge upon any innocent in order to assuage his wrath, accusing someone of being a traitor and making a sport of his torture and death? He had done horrid things such as this in the past. Or would he blame Lanos for the way he had conducted the attack and accuse him perhaps of giving some indication to the enemy, giving them time to escape? But how could that be? They were stealthily quiet, and very quick. He had done everything he could to ensure the element of surprise. All of a sudden he felt less than the mighty general that he was esteemed to be; he felt confused, afraid and very, very small. The only thing to do was to...

"Ride on to Phyladel!" he barked the order to his bewildered troops. "Obviously the enemy was somehow alerted to our attack and is afraid and on the run for the shelter of the nearest city. We will pursue and overtake them while they are still in flight and then continue on to slay all the inhabitants of the city. No time to waste! Ride on! Ride on!" He gave his mare a hard kick in the side and led the companies of soldiers swiftly through the Fields of Jaar in the direction of the capitol city.

CHAPTER XIII
The Reign of Terror

"Try the next house!" shouted Lanos angrily. A couple of soldiers ran down the dark cobblestone street to yet another one of the houses which lined the avenue that wound it's way from the city gates to the great castle.

When they had arrived at the gates of Phyladel, they were perplexed that they found them completely unguarded. Lanos had ordered fifty of his men to climb the wall, overtake the guards and open the gates to let in the remaining troops. But the men found the guard posts completely vacant. Once they opened the gates, the rest of the army had swarmed the city like thousands of blood-thirsty locusts and quickly began their house-to-house mission of evil.

Lanos' command when they had first arrived in Phyladel had been *very* clear. "I want them *all* dead, down to the smallest baby in his crib—Darius's orders! The man who shows mercy will himself find *none*!" had been his directive. But now ... where were all the people?

"I'm sorry, sir. No one here either," came the lieutenant's tentative reply after several minutes of searching yet another stone house. This was the fifty-first house they had searched, but all to no avail. They were finding the same sort of strange things here as they had back in the enemy camp. Fires were still lit in fireplaces with pots of food on the hearth; plates of half-eaten food were still on the tables.

"Is there some *problem* with my orders?!" Chills went up the general's spine as he heard Darius's hissing voice close behind him.

Lanos quickly spun on his heels. "No, My Lord! We are trying with all our might to carry out your instructions. It's just that...well, they all appear to be...gone."

Darius had been greatly displeased when he reached the abandoned enemy camp and saw no signs whatsoever that there was any spilling of blood. He and his men had ridden quickly on to catch up with the army in Phyladel. But what Darius found here was equally as disturbing.

"What exactly do you mean by 'they all appear to be gone'!? Gone WHERE!" he screamed in fury. "Where could an entire city of people mysteriously *disappear* to in the middle of the night?! Lanos, find out who tipped them off and bring him to me. I would hate to think that any of the fault for the failure of this mission lay with you, General," he hissed, his narrowed eyes boring a hole right through his second-in-command. "For now, we go to the castle to see what we find there. We will seize the building and make it our new headquarters. I will take my seat on the throne of my enemy and reign from there over the entire continent of Austire!"

They arrived at the palace to find it, to no one's surprise at this point, quite deserted. They hurried through the corridors and hallways on the main level, checking every room for those that may have been left behind when the others fled.

Darius himself, with a small band of men, was the first to throw open the great doors of the throne room. He and his men were perplexed by what they found there. There were cots intermittent from one end of the room to the other, some overturned, some upright. Most of the sheets that covered them had been stained with blood. They found surgical trays and instruments strewn all over the floor amid broken glass and pottery fragments. Spanning the entire length of the room, from the great doors in the rear all the way up to the throne itself, ran a wide crack in the solid marble floor. The opening was at least one foot wide in most places and about the same in depth. While it was obvious that the great chamber had been being used as a medical facility, what chaotic event had transpired here was beyond anyone's guess. Darius and Lanos looked at one another for an explanation, but there was none.

"You five over there," the evil lord said, pointing to a group of soldiers, "clean up this place and make it ready for the *new* king to take the throne! Everyone else, continue your search under General Lanos's oversight on the other levels of the building." He turned to Lanos. "I'll be outside if you find anything. Oh, and General," he patted Lanos's back with mock affection. "It would be in your best interest not to let me down again." Lanos got his meaning loud and clear.

The search party continued through the many corridors of the upper floor of Calla Alesse. They found no one — except, that is, for one person. His name was Zantar, and he was a spy whom Darius had planted in the palace several years earlier, just as he had Mari. Mari had helped to maintain the beautiful gardens surrounding the estate, and Zantar had been given a job assisting with the upkeep of the palace interior. Lanos found Zantar fast asleep in his chamber on the far right wing of the upper level of the building.

"Zantar, get out of bed, you fool!!! And you had better have some answers for us!"

Zantar started, wakened abruptly out of his deep sleep.

94

"What? What? Who is it?" The disoriented spy rubbed his eyes, trying to help them adjust to the bright light of the torches which now blinded the bewildered man.

Lanos brought his face closer, glaring at the timid-looking man in the bed. "General!" he exclaimed, jumping abruptly, and rather clumsily, to his feet and standing at attention.

"What in the world happened here, Zantar?!"

"I...I don't know what you mean, sir. Nothing has happened that has been out of the ordinary for wartime. They have just set up a hospital downstairs and are working on their wounded as they come in from the field. But other than that, I haven't noticed anything worthy of reporting to His Majes—"

"No, man! I mean where has everyone gone?"

"I don't know what you are talking about, sir. Who is gone?"

"*Everyone* is gone, you idiot! *Everyone!!!*" Lanos spun on his heels. "Guards, bring him!" he snapped over his shoulder.

Lanos brought the spy to Darius for further questioning. The stout, awkward little traitor, still in his nightshirt, was now visibly shaking, no matter how hard he tried to look like he was being brave. He knew that his life was in the hands of tyrants who would just as soon kill him for sneezing the wrong way as for any serious infraction of his commander's orders.

"He seems to know nothing about the disappearance, my lord. He appears to be telling the truth and to be just as baffled as we are."

"I'll be the judge of who's telling the truth!" bellowed Darius.

"Yes, sir."

"What other spies have we in the city?"

"Well, sir, there are Thomas and Logan, then there's —"

Darius cut him off abruptly mid-sentence. "Go check all of *their* homes as well and bring to me *anyone* you find there, immediately!"

Lanos and his men returned three hours later with five spies and their families that had been planted in Phyladel. It was obvious that all of them had been dragged out of their beds. Lanos motioned for Zantar to join the group.

"This is all of the spies we had in the city. They are all accounted for," reported Lanos.

Darius walked up and down the line-up, interrogating each person in a very intimidating and accusing manner.

"How is it that *none* of you got word to us that the enemy was preparing to leave the city? You can't tell me *none* of you knew about it, that none of you at least heard *stirrings* of such an event. You were supposed to *blend in* and pretend to be *one* of them. Surely they would have told you of the plans of the ENTIRE CITY to FLEE!!! And, how does an entire city leave in the middle of the night and YOU NOT KNOW ABOUT IT!!!"

Here he lowered his voice and rubbed his chin with his hand thoughtfully. "But I am actually leaning toward my second theory. I think that one of you had to have betrayed our plans to the enemy. Which one of you was it?" But each one denied it in turn, declaring adamantly that they knew nothing of the escape by night, nor did they turn over any plans.

"Alright then, if that's the way we're going to play it," Darius turned to Lanos. "Kill them all," he said flatly.

Deafening his ears to the cries for mercy and the declarations of innocence and loyalty, Lanos carried out the terrible orders. He was just relieved that Darius had found another scapegoat--or scapegoats--and that *he* was off the hook...for now.

As the next couple of days unfolded, the unexplainable disappearance became more and more mysterious. Assuming that all of the residents of Phyladel had fled to one of the other Orzanian cities, Darius sent squadrons of men to each of the remaining six provinces to assess the situation. But each came back in turn reporting that these cities, as well, were almost entirely vacated. They had even checked the harbors in all of the coastal cities, assuming that the residents must have fled by ship. But from all appearances, the entire fleet was still intact. What they found in each city was that only their own spies, as well as some of the residents who had not fully pledged their allegiance to King Reagale and his father, remained.

What they also found in these cities was widespread panic, especially amidst those who had relations which were among the missing. The people who were left appeared to be completely and legitimately unaware of the whereabouts of the others. Terror gripped their hearts as they searched for answers to a situation which offered none. Reports came back to Darius that the people who remained were in utter chaos and mass hysteria. There was extensive looting occurring, as well as rioting and other unlawful behavior.

"I am half-tempted to allow the lawlessness to continue and just let the little maggots kill themselves off," he said to his top officials. "But I really can't do that, you see, because I need the handful of people that are left to work the land for me here, just as the pathetic peasants do in Trenza." He stroked his straggly beard thoughtfully. "So, I suppose we have to keep at least *most* of them alive. However," he slammed his fist down on the large oak table with force and rose to his feet, "let it be known that *anyone* who speaks the name of King Reagale Constance or Emperor Liam is to be executed immediately!" He stopped his ranting for a moment and looked pensive. "On second thought, don't kill them immediately. Bring them here to me so that I can personally watch the complete annihilation of every single follower of the King of Orza!" he spat venomously.

But Darius's troubles were far from over, and victory was much further from his grasp than he realized. The Vanishing, as it had come to be called, was by far the least of his worries. Although he claimed sure victory, deadly challenges lay just around the corner and out of his sight. Although he would win some battles along the way, he could not escape the fate that awaited him in the days to come. The evil that he had been unleashing so viciously upon so many helpless victims would soon come back to him in immeasurable quantities and with greater horror than he could possibly imagine...

Dear Reader,

I hope you enjoyed Volume II of *The Orphan and the King* series, <u>*Love's Great Ransom*</u>. Perhaps you read it simply as a story of fiction, with no real relevance or importance for your life today. But I hope and pray that something deeper and more wonderful happened, or may even at this moment be happening, in your heart.

Did you find *yourself* in the pages of this book? Were you able to see yourself in any of the characters?

Perhaps you identified a bit with Mari. You have known of the goodness and kindness of the great King, Jesus, and have enjoyed the bounty and abundance of His house and table but have since turned and walked away. I believe the Lord would say to you today that this doesn't have to be the end for you. He is calling you to come back, and He waits for you with open arms of love and forgiveness. Simply turn from your sin and return to your loving and compassionate King and let today mark, not a tragic end, but rather a new and wonderful beginning.

Maybe you have lived your whole life disbelieving in the goodness of, or even the very existence of, the King. Perhaps He has been grossly misrepresented to you by others, maybe even by 'religious' people. Maybe the 'King' that they have told you of, or tried to make known to you, was either utterly detestable and loathsome to you or was a pitiful, pathetic figure not worthy of your allegiance. Come today to the *true* King, for He will neither disappoint you nor fail you!

<u>How to Receive Christ</u>

1. Admit your sin *(wrongdoing or disobedience toward God and His Word, not valuing God as He deserves)* and your need of a Savior.

2. Be willing to turn from your sins *(repent)*. Ask God for His help.

3. Believe that Jesus Christ died for you on the cross, taking the punishment that you deserved for your sins, so that you could have peace with God, who is completely holy and sinless. There is no way you could ever earn this great gift of salvation, because it is not bought by good works, so that no one can boast in their own deeds or merits. It is the gift of God (read Ephesians 2:8-9, Isaiah 64:6, Romans 3:10-12, Romans 3:22-28).

4. Through prayer, invite Jesus Christ to come in and control your life through the Holy Spirit *(receive Him as your Savior and King)*.

Pray:

Dear Lord Jesus, I know that I am sinful and I need Your forgiveness. I believe that You died to pay the penalty for my sin. I want to turn from my sin and follow You instead. I invite You to come into my heart and life. In Jesus' name, Amen!

What Now?

1. Talk to God each day, which will help your relationship with Him to grow.

2. Spend time reading His Word, the Bible. Start with the book of John.

3. Tell others that you took this important step to turn your life over to Christ.

4. Find a good, Bible-believing church and get involved.

If you have just prayed this prayer to turn your will and your life over to Jesus and to trust Him as your Savior, or if you have any questions about what you've read, please call us and let us know! We want to send you free literature to help you grow in your new relationship with God!

1-866-782-7927

Please let me know what this book has meant to you:

WendyAnneHunt@comcast.net
www.HuntandPeckPress.com

Free Bonus Items!

- *Free* downloadable extensive vocabulary and spelling *Study Guide* based on the book! (extensive, color, reproducible)

- *Free* downloadable *Video Art Lesson* from Emmy-nominated television cartoonist Bruce Blitz!

To obtain downloads, simply go to:

www.HuntandPeckPress.com

Glossary

Of Words, Phrases and Non-Traditional Meanings

abbreviated – shortened
abounding – plentiful, containing something in large quantities
abruptly – suddenly, unexpectedly
accounted for – making sure every person or thing in a group is
        there
accurate – correct, true
accustomed – used to, familiar with, comfortable
adamantly – stubbornly, unbendingly
advances – to press forward, to move ahead
affairs – dealings, important personal matters
alert – watchful
allegations – to blame or make accusations against another
allegiance – devotion to
altitude – height
anguish – suffering, pain, sorrow
annihilation – total destruction
anticipation – hope, eagerness
anxiously – fearfully, worriedly
appease – calm, soothe, ease
appointed – chosen
artifacts – an object made by a human being
ascent – climb
ashen – pale
assembled – gathered
assess – examine something in order to evaluate or judge it
assuage – ease, soften, relieve
astonishment – surprise, shock
at stake – at risk, in danger
attempt – try
attire – clothing
audience – meeting
authoritative – trustworthy, dependable
authority – power

await – wait for
awe – wonder, amazement
awkward – clumsy, uncoordinated
babbling – bubbling water
baffled – puzzled, confused
balm – healing ointment or cream
barred – banned, would not allow
barren – deserted
battalion – troop (i.e. of soldiers)
battened down – secured, fastened down
battered – beaten-up
beady – small, round, and shiny like a bead
beamed – smiled widely
bear – to be marked with, show, display
beckoned – called to
bellowing – shouting, yelling
beloved – dearly loved
bestowed – given
betrayer – traitor
bewildered – confused
beyond measure – too great to be measured
bidding – request, command, order, will
bitter – unpleasant
bleaker – without hope or expectation of success or improvement
boisterously – rowdily, noisily, wildly
boring – making holes in things
bough – branch, limb
bounded – leapt
bounty – abundant supply
breathtaking – spectacular, awesome
brilliant – bright, dazzling
broached – brought up, mentioned
broad – wide, large
brow – forehead or temple
brutish – rough, uncivilized, wild

budge – move, push, shove

canvas – heavy fabric

capricious – tending to make sudden unexpected changes

captivity – a period of time that someone is held prisoner

caressed – gently touched, affectionately embraced someone

catacombs – network of tunnels below ground

cautiously – carefully

ceased – ended

centerpiece – showpiece, focal point of a room or table

central – innermost, middle

chambers – rooms

chaotic – confused, hectic, frenzied, unruly

chided – to bring gentle correction, sometimes playfully

chimed – to say something or speak in a rhythmic or musical way

civilians – non-soldiers, regular citizens

clamored – causing a commotion or racket

coarse – rough

coastal – found along the coast of a country, state or province

coaxed – encouraged, urged

cobblestone – small rounded paving stone

collapsed – fell down

combat – fighting, especially between armies

commemorate – to remember or honor something or someone with a ceremony

commenced – began

commerce – large-scale buying and selling of goods and services

commissioned – an instruction to do something

commissioning – appointment as a military officer

commotion – disturbance, uproar

communicate – to talk, to be in contact with

company – group

competitive – spirited, lively

conch shell – large spiral shell

condemn – to say somebody or something is bad

conducted – carried out, managed, or controlled something

conniving – devious and scheming

conquest – invasion, take-over

consequences – penalties

consoled – cheered up, comforted

constituted authorities – formally established government officials

contemporaries – somebody existing during the same period of time as another, someone of about the same age as someone else

contemplate – consider something thoughtfully, to think about

contrasted – was very different than something else

conveyed – told, expressed

convoy – group, band of people

core of his being – the central part of a person

corridor – hallway, passageway

cosmic – vast, far-reaching, global

course through – run through, move through

courtyard – plaza, open area

covenant – agreement, contract, treaty, promise, pledge

cover – disguise, camouflage

cowardly – weak, gutless

crag – rock face, overhang, precipice

crest – top, peak

critical – important, significant

crouch – squat, bend down, duck

crude – rough, unfinished, makeshift

cumbersome – bulky, awkward

cut-to-the-quick – emotionally moved in the heart in a negative way

dashing – shattering, breaking

decaying – rotting

deliberately – with intent, calculatingly, slowly

delicately – carefully

designated – chosen, selected

despair – depression, misery, hopelessness

desperate – frantic, worried, distressed, anxious

despondency – sadness, gloom, misery, hopelessness

destitute – poor, penniless, needy, impoverished

detestable – unpleasant, vile, revolting

devastating – dreadful, overwhelming

devotion – attachment, loyalty

dewy – moist, covered with dew

dictator – powerful ruler

dignitary – someone who holds a high rank or position

disdain – extreme contempt or disgust for someone or something

disfigured – spoiled or marred in appearance

disheveled – with messed-up hair or clothes

dismal – miserable, gloomy, dreary, bleak

dismissed – to send someone away or allow them to leave

dismounted – to get off an animal

dispersed – scattered

displayed – demonstrated

dissonant – harsh sound, unmusical, not harmonious

dormer – a portion of roof projecting out from main roof and covering a window

dousing – drenching, soaking, saturating

downhearted – sad, discouraged

drapes – long curtains

drawn – closed

drawn up – written up

dreadful – terrible

dreariness – bleakness, cheerlessness, gloominess

dreary – bleak, dismal, miserable

drenched – soaked, very wet

drizzle – sprinkle, light rain

dub – to call, to name, to hail as

dwell – live, stay, reside

eagerly – excitedly, enthusiastically

earnestly – sincerely, intently, seriously

eerie – sinister, ghostlike, creepy

eerily – sinisterly, creepily, strangely

element of surprise – the ability to catch someone or something
    unawares

elevated – raised

embankment – mound, edge

embarked – to start out upon a journey

embedded – fixed, set in, implanted

embers – remains of a fire, burning fragments

emblem – symbol or image

embraced – hugged

emerged – came out

emphatic – forceful

enchanted – mystical, under a spell

encompassed – included

endure – bear, tolerate

engage – fight somebody

engrave – to imprint something

engulfed – overwhelmed, surrounded

enhancing – improving

enormity – vastness, hugeness, sheer size

enrobed – dressed grandly

enthusiasm – eagerness, zeal, excitement

entryway – entrance, door, front entrance

erupted – burst out

esteemed – regarded, admired, valued

evergreen bush – a bush that keeps its foliage/leaves all year

exact – to inflict something as suffering

exasperatedly – in a frustrated or angry way

excess – extra, leftover

executioner – killer, assassin

exhaustion – overtiredness

exhilarating – exciting, thrilling

expansive – wide, spacious, large

expeditions – journeys, trips

exploit – misuse, abuse, take advantage of

exposed – uncovered, revealed, made known, found out

extensive – far-reaching, widespread

famed – famous, celebrated, legendary

fared – to get on in a particular way in doing or experiencing
      something

fate – destiny, lot in life, future, end

fateful – tragic, ill-fated, ominous

feeble – weak

fell – destroy, take out

fend off – hold off

ferociously – brutally, violently, fiercely

fertility – fruitfulness, lushness

festivities – celebrations, merriment, partying

filed up – walked up single file in a line

finalized – settled, completed

fleet – navy, convoy, task force

flimsy – light, thin and easily torn

flush – redness, to blush

flustered – tense, uncomfortable, ill at ease, upset

foe – enemy

foreboding – ominous, menacing, threatening, sinister

forefinger – same as index finger

forged – to develop something with great effort

for good measure – as a bonus, an unexpected extra thing given

formally – officially

fortified – prepared, equipped, made stronger

foundation – base, support for a building

fragments – rubble, wreckage, remains

frantically – worriedly, hysterically, crazily

fret – worry, upset, trouble

frolicked – played

fulfilled – achieved, completed, come to be

full-fledged – full grown, adult

funneled – channeled, directed

furiously – at high speed

furtherance – advancement

futile – useless, unsuccessful, pointless

gay – happy, joyful

gauze – loosely woven fabric used for covering wounds

gaze – look, stare

gestured – motioned

get their bearings – to find out where you are or where you are going after being lost or confused

glaring – staring angrily

gloom – despair, misery, dreariness

gnawing – distressing, concerning, worrisome

got his wits about him – was able to think clearly

gracing – to contribute something pleasing

grasp – understand

grave – serious, severe

gravity – seriousness, magnitude, severity

grief – sorrow, heartache, pain, misery

grieve – mourn, be sad

groped – fumbled about, felt around for

grossly – largely

grove – orchard, woods

grueling – demanding, exhausting, severe, backbreaking, very hard

gruesome – horrible, dreadful

gust – blast of air

gutter – sewer, drain

half-mast – lowered flag honoring dead person

half-pence – a very small unit of money

hallucination – illusion, figment of the imagination, vision, fantasy

haste – rush, quickness

haunting – lingering, unforgettable

heart-wrenching – causing someone to feel very sad or distressed

hearty – enthusiastic, wholehearted

heaving – alternately rising and falling

heir – legal inheritor of something, successor

hemming it in – creating boundaries or borders

hemp – tough fiber from Asian plant

herded – steered, directed

hesitation – uncertainty, pause or delay

hewn – cut down

hideousness – ugliness, repulsiveness

high-ranking – important, superior

hitching posts – a post used to tie horses to

hodgepodge – mishmash, jumble, mixture

hoisted – lifted, raised, pulled up

honored – pleased, grateful, thrilled, privileged, flattered

hopelessness – despair, depression

horrid – terrible, hideous, dreadful

hovered – floated, flew

hushed – quiet

hysteria – panic

hysterically – uncontrollable, wildly, desperately

identified – related to, felt a connection or similarity to

immeasurable – unable to be measured, endless, massive

immense – huge, enormous, giant

imminent – about to happen

immovable – unbending, stubborn, firm, steadfast

impact – force, shock

impenetrable – unable to get in or through

implement – put into action, apply

imposing – intimidating, scary, overwhelming

imprint – dent, indentation or mark on something

improbability – not likely

inconsolably – so sad that no one can bring comfort

incredulously – in amazement, in disbelief

in cruel fashion – in a brutal, vicious, or mean way

indicate – show, imply, reveal

indication – sign, signal, warning, clue

indisputable – beyond all doubt, certain

indoctrinated – trained, instructed, programmed

induced – caused, brought about

in due time – at the proper or appropriate time

in essence – for the most part, pretty much

inevitable – inescapable, unavoidable, predictable, expected

infiltrate – enter enemy territory secretly

informant – spy

informed – notified, made aware of something

infraction – failure to obey or fulfill a law, contract or agreement

injustice – unfairness, wrong

inland – not near coast or border

inmate – prisoner

inquisitively – curiously, questioningly

in royal fashion – in an extravagant, magnificent way

insight – ability to see clearly into nature of complex person, situation or subject

intensity – force, power, amount

intent – goal, plan

intentions – goals, plans

intently – carefully, closely

interfere – intervene, get involved

interjected – butted in, interrupted

intermittent – sporadic, at irregular intervals

internally – inside, within

interrogating – questioning, cross-examining

intimidating – threatening, frightening

in turn – in order

in vain – pointlessly, unsuccessfully

irony – a twist of fate

irrational – silly, absurd, not making sense

irregular – random, fitful

jagged – uneven, toothed

jeering – mocking, name calling

jurisdiction – authority, control

justify – give a reason for, excuse, defend

keen – well developed, sharp, perceptive

laid bare – exposed, made known

landing – floor at top or foot of a flight of stairs

launch – begin a carefully planned activity

legitimate – legal, genuine, valid, rightful

legitimately – truly, really, truthfully

liberation – freedom

lilting – a pleasant rising and falling variation in the pitch of a person's voice; a cheerful song

limb – branch

limp – floppy, drooping, lifeless

lingered – remained

literature – writing, text

loathsome – detestable, hateful

looting – stealing valuables during a time of disorder or confusion

lumber – wood or timber used for building

maggots – people who are despised; the worm-shaped larva of various members of the fly family, found in decaying matter

magnified – increased in size or importance

makeshift – a temporary and usually lower quality substitute for something

managing – organizing, running, supervising

manifestation – demonstration, appearance, materialization

mare – stallion, steed

marked – was very noticeable

mass – crowd, large group

matted – tangled, messed up, knotted

matter – subject, topic, issue

meager – skimpy, small, measly, not enough, too little

meditate – consider, think about, ponder

melody – tune, song

memoirs – journals, accounts, records

menacing – scary, frightening, threatening

mercilessly – cruelly, without pity, unkindly

mercenaries – private army, band of soldiers

merrymaking – laughter, amusement, joyfulness, cheer

midsection – area of body between chest and waist

military – army

mingled – mixed in

minstrels – medieval-type musicians or singers who traveled around from place to place giving performances

mislaid – lost, misplaced

misrepresented – to give an inaccurate or false account of the nature of someone or something

mobilized – organized, assembled, gathered together

mock – fake

mocking – teasing, making fun of

monarch – ruler

motley – made up of very different types that don't seem to belong together

mounted – got on

mounting – rising, increasing

mourning – grief, sorrow over the loss of someone or something

muffled – sounding less loud, quieter

mussed – messed up

muster – gather, get together

narrow – thin, tight

navigating – finding the way

noble – dignified, impressive in quality or appearance

no force to be reckoned with – to be avoided regarding conflict

noose – loop in a rope

obstructing – getting in the way, blocking, hindering

occasion – event

occasional – something taking place once in a while at random periods of time

offensive – attack

omnipotent – all-powerful

on his behalf – for him, in his place

onlookers – observers, bystanders

onset – beginning, start of something

opposing – competing, rival, challenging, opposite

outrage – anger, fury

outskirts – outer edge, border

overturned – turned upside down

overwhelmed – weighed down, overpowered by emotion

pale – white, colorless, indicator of sickness or fear

panicked – sudden feeling of extreme fear or anxiety

parchment – former writing material of dried animal hide

particular – specific, exact

pathetic – pitiful, weak, useless

peered – looked intently

penalty – punishment

penetrating – piercing, stabbing

pensively – thoughtfully

perimeter – a boundary or border that encloses an area

perplexed – confused

perplexing – confusing

persevere – continue, stick with it, keep trying

petition – beg, plead

piped in – said, stated, added

pitiful – pathetic, poor

placate – soothe, calm

plane – level of reality

plateau – flat, raised ground

plight – troubles, difficulty

poised – prepared

portrait – description, picture

posed – asked

posthaste – as quickly as possible

precipice – rock face, cliff, sheer drop

pre-emptive – defensive, in order to prevent something

prelude – introduction to something else usually longer and more
        important

present – there, in attendance

presumed – believed

prevent – stop

previous – earlier, before

previously – beforehand, in the past

prey – victim

principles – a set of standards, beliefs or values

prior – earlier, before

proceeded – advanced, went on

process – deal with, handle

prodded – jabbed, pushed

prognosis – prediction about how a situation will turn out

progress – move forward, develop, evolve

pronouncement – declaration, statement, announcement, decree

propose – suggest

public arena – community at large

purposeful – decided, with firm determination

quaking – trembling, quivering, shaking

quantities – numbers

quiver – long narrow case for holding arrows

radiating – glowing, shining

rancid – rotten

randomly – without a plan or pattern

rank – status, position, title

ranks – lines of people or things

ransacked – searched, went through

rasped – said something in a harsh voice

raspy – harsh sounding

ravaging – damaging, destructive

ravine – narrow valley, gully, canyon

reasoned – thought in a logical way

reassuring – comforting, encouraging, supportive

reattach – to fasten together again

recall – remember

recounted – told, described

reflected – thought seriously about, pondered

refuge – shelter, place of safety

regained his composure – took control back over his emotions

regroup – change around, rearrange

rehearsed – practiced

relevance – importance
relieve – fire someone from a job or position
remembrance – memory
reminisced – talked about, recalled, brought to mind
remorse – regret, guilt, shame
rendered – made to be
reservation – hesitation
resistance – opposition, refusal to go along with
resolve – determination
restrain – hold back, control
resumed – continued
retribution – revenge
reunion – get-together, meeting
revelry – festivities, celebration
reverent – respectful, in awe
reversal – turnaround
rhythm – beat, tempo
ritual – formal procedure, custom, tradition
ruffled – to disturb or ripple something, messed up
salve – ointment, cream, balm
satchel – shoulder bag
scapegoat – somebody made to take the blame for others
scarcely – barely, not quite
scarred – bearing a scar, disfigured, marked
scattered – few in number and far apart
scenarios – situations, circumstances
scenic – lovely, beautiful
sculptured – 3D work or art created especially by carving,
        modeling, or casting
securing – attaching firmly
seemingly – outwardly, apparently
seize – grab hold of, take control of
semi-bleary-eyed – half-awake, sleepy, drowsy, tired, groggy
senses – the 5 senses of sight, smell, taste, touch, and hearing
shackles – chains

shards – broken pieces of glass or metal

sheath – case

sheepish – embarrassed

sheer – pure, absolute, complete, total

shimmering – shining with wavering light

shredding – ripping, pulling something apart

significant – major, noteworthy, large

signify – be a sign of, show, imply

sinister – evil, creepy, threatening

sizeable – large

slain – killed

slaughter – kill, murder, massacre

slavery – a state of being completely under enemy control

slumped – collapsed, sank or fell suddenly and heavily

smugly – arrogantly, self-importantly, in a prideful way

soft – weak, spineless

solemn – sad, serious

solidify – make firm

soothe – ease pain, relieve

sorely – deeply, very much

sought – wanted, hunted for

soul – heart, core of one's being

source – informer, supplier of information

sovereigns – royals, monarchs

span – width or length, distance

spectacle – display, show, sight, demonstration

spectacular – magnificent, marvelous, incredible

speculated – guessed

squadron – troop, squad

staggering – shocking, incredible, unbelievable

staggers the imagination – is difficult to even imagine

stale – not fresh

stallion – horse

stammered – stumbled over their words, spoke with hesitations
     and repeated words

stark – complete, total

started – to make a sudden movement out of surprise, pain, fear or anger

stature – size, tallness, height, build

steadfast – dedicated, committed, firm, unwavering

stealthy – secret, sly, sneaky, cautious

steed – horse

steely – determined, firm, unbending, tough

stench – stink, disgusting odor

stern – unsympathetic, hardhearted, firm

stirrings – murmurings, whispers

stole – to go quietly, especially in the hope of not being seen or caught

stout – fat

straddling – with a leg on each side of something

straggly – messy, untidy, scruffy

strained – made extreme effort

strategically – deliberately, intentionally, purposefully

strategy – plan

street urchin – very messy, bratty child who lives on the street

stretcher – device for carrying someone who is lying down because of sickness, injury or death

strewn – scattered

structures – buildings

stunned – amazed, surprised

summon – call

suppress – hold back

surge – flood, outpouring

surly – bad-tempered

sustain – keep you going

swarmed – mobbed, flooded into

swift – very quick

symbolically – acting as a symbol of something else, representing something else

sympathy – pity

tactics – plans, strategies

talents – abilities, areas of gifting

tangible – something that has a physical form, can be touched

tarnish – dullness or discoloration of metal

tarry – wait, delay

tattered – torn, in rags, shabby

taunted – tease, insult, mock

tempo – rhythm, beat

tenacious – persistent, determined, steadfast

tended – taken care of

tentative – hesitant, cautious, unsure

territory – regions, provinces, land

theory – assumption, speculation, educated guess, thought

thicket – grove, wood, orchard

thugs – brutes, tough guys

tinged – colored

tipped them off – gave them advice

togs - shorts

toil – work

toting – carrying

traditional sense of the word – the most commonly used meaning
    of a word

tragedy – disaster

traitor – double agent, spy

transpired – happened

treachery – betrayal, disloyalty

treated – cared for

treatment center – medical center, hospital

trickled – dripped, oozed

trifle – a little bit

tumultuous – disorderly, chaotic, riotous

turbulence – gusty, unpredictable air currents

turn in – go to bed

twisted pleasure – cruel enjoyment

tyrants – tormenters, bullies

unbridled – not held back, unrestrained, openly expressed

uncommon – rare, unusual

unconscious – experiencing loss of senses due to accident or injury

undercurrent – a current in a body of water that flows beneath another current or beneath the surface of the water

undying – never-ending

unflinchingly – without fear, courageously

unfolded – developed

unhindered – not blocked by anything

unleashing – letting loose

unmistakable – easily recognized

unmistakably – obviously

unnerved – unsettled, upset, intimidated

unrelentingly – without weakening or easing up

unrepentant – not sorry or ashamed

unsightly – ugly, unpleasant, horrid

untouchable – unpleasant or disagreeable to touch

upright – standing vertically or straight upward rather than at an angle or turned over

utter – say

vacant – empty

valiant – brave, heroic, fearless

valor – bravery, fearlessness

variation – change

vast – huge, enormous

veered – turned

vengeance – punishment, revenge

vengeful – ruthless, merciless

venomously – cruelly, bitterly

ventured – made a trip that is unpleasant or dangerous

vicious – cruel, nasty, mean

vigorously – energetically

visibly – obviously, noticeably

vision – dream, hallucination

voluntarily – willingly

vulnerable – helpless, at risk, weak

wail – cry

warred – battled

was birthed – had its start, came into being

wed – get married

well-kempt – neat, cared for

whatsoever – at all

wheezed – rasped, hissed

whereabouts – location, position

whim – sudden thought, idea, or desire

whisked – to make someone move somewhere quickly or suddenly

widespread – affecting many people

winded – out of breath

with a start – with a jerk or a twitch

yielded – brought forth, produce

Author Biography

Wendy Anne Hunt lives in southern New Jersey with her wonderful husband and three delightful children. Because of her passion for 'redemptive writing' that points others to the cross and the Savior, Hunt is happiest when putting pen to paper—whether writing music, weaving a story, writing poetry or working on a book in progress. Her hope is that God would use these means to draw the hearts of others nearer to the Lord she loves.

Books in Print

The Orphan and the King, Volume I: *The Freedom Mission*
The Orphan and the King, Volume II: *Love's Great Ransom*

Other Books Coming Soon

The Orphan and the King, Volume III: *The Final Conquest*

Whispers of Grace:
Tender Words from the Father for the Daily Refreshment
of His Children

Breinigsville, PA USA
20 May 2010
238365BV00001B/7/P